THE COMFORT OF STRANGERS

When Carrie Martin's family falls on hard times, she struggles to support her frail sister and inadequate father. While scavenging along the shoreline of the Thames for firewood, she stumbles over the unconscious body of a young man. As she nurses him back to health she falls in love with the stranger. But there is a mystery surrounding the identity of 'Mr Jones' and, as Carrie tries to find out who he really is, she finds herself in danger.

Books by Roberta Grieve
in the Linford Romance Library:

A HATFUL OF DREAMS

ROBERTA GRIEVE

THE COMFORT OF STRANGERS

Complete and Unabridged

LINFORD
Leicester

First published in Great Britain in 2006

First Linford Edition
published 2008

British Library CIP Data

Grieve, Roberta
    The comfort of strangers.—Large print ed.—
Linford romance library
    1. Poor—Fiction 2. London (England)—
Fiction 3. Love stories 4. Large type books
I. Title
823.9′2 [F]

ISBN 978–1–84782–105–8

Published by
F. A. Thorpe (Publishing)
Anstey, Leicestershire

Set by Words & Graphics Ltd.
Anstey, Leicestershire
Printed and bound in Great Britain by
T. J. International Ltd., Padstow, Cornwall

This book is printed on acid-free paper

1

The sulphurous fog swirled through the narrow streets, almost blocking out the light from the gas lamps and hiding the passers-by. At this hour of the night, when in happier times she would have been snugly tucked up in bed, Carrie Martin was surprised that there were so many people about. The muffled clop of horses pulling cabs and heavy drays and the hoarse shouts of the drunks leaving the tavern on the corner came faintly through the thick, almost unbreathable air.

Carrie coughed and pulled her shawl more closely around her. Glancing round, she slipped quietly out of the narrow entrance to Brewers Court and, keeping close to the walls of the houses, felt her way along the street.

The fog, while frightening in its all-enveloping density, was a blessing in

1

a way. She need not fear being seen on her shameful errand. Would she ever get used to this dreadful way of life?

She sighed. There was no way out. She'd have to try and make the best of things as she had been learning to do over the past couple of years as their fortunes had gradually declined.

Before her mother died, Carrie had been happy, her days filled, it seemed now, with sunshine and laughter. She and her sister had sung and played the piano. Entertained friends in the beautifully-furnished drawing-room, danced the nights away at balls and parties.

A figure loomed up out of the fog and Carrie stared back in alarm, her thoughts of her previous life abruptly banished. She should keep her wits about her. Dreadful things could happen to a girl out at night on her own, especially round here where sailors from the docks were looking to spend their money on booze and women.

'Eh, Carrie, duck — it is you, isn't

it?' Faint light from an overhead gas lamp illuminated the painted face, the hat with its feather over one eye, the peacock blue fringed shawl, and Carrie recognised her neighbour.

'Nancy, you startled me,' she gasped.

'What you doin' out in this weather, gel. You'll catch your death.' Nancy put a hand on the other girl's arm and gave a screech of laughter. 'Eh, you ain't decided to go on the game too, 'ave yer?'

Carrie shook the hand off. 'Of course I haven't. What do you take me for?' She was immediately ashamed of her reaction. 'I'm sorry, Nancy. I shouldn't have said that.'

The young woman shrugged. 'Don't mind me.'

Carrie drew back into the darkness and continued on her way. As she got nearer to the river, the stench of rotting vegetation and worse told her that the tide was out. She was beginning to know the Thames like a native Londoner. She hurried on to the wharf and climbed down the slippery weed-strewn steps.

Others were here before her, scurrying figures, carrying torches of rags dipped in tar. She hoped there was something left for her, cursing the delay caused by the fog and stopping to talk to Nancy.

Along the tide line, heaps of refuse were being turned over by the gang of boys known as mudlarks. She was a mudlark too now. The boys were after rich pickings, anything they could sell such as nails and lumps of iron, as well as pieces of coal which fell from the ships as they were being unloaded. Sometimes they were lucky enough to find coins or items of jewellery lost overboard from the ferries which piled between the big ships and the wharves.

All Carrie wanted was fuel for the fire, coal and pieces of tarry driftwood which would warm the hovel they now called home. The two-roomed house in the little court off Wapping High Street was the latest and — Carrie hoped

4

— the last in a series of moves that had taken them ever further from their roots in their descent into poverty.

She tried not to blame her father. Josiah Martin had been so devastated by the death of his wife that he had lost all interest in his business, spending his days slumped in a chair, a bottle at his side. But she could not help feeling a spurt of anger towards him as she thought of her young sister, Eliza, who each day seemed to slip further into decline.

She already had as much fuel wrapped in her shawl as she could carry. She had kept away from the gang of boys, not wanting them to think she was poaching on their territory.

The fog parted as a breeze drifted upriver, bringing a faint smell of the sea. The tide was turning and she would have to hurry.

The boys were still at the water's edge, poking at something which moved sluggishly as the rising tide crept across the mud.

''E's dead, ain't 'e?' she heard one of them say.

'Ain't worth nothing to us dead,' another replied.

'Nothin' in 'is pockets neither.' Carrie recognised the voice of Jerry, the boy who lived across the court. He was the one who'd told her about mudlarking and how, on a good night, they could make enough money to keep themselves for a week.

As low as she'd fallen in the past months, Carrie still felt shocked that they would think of robbing the dead, although common sense told her the man's belongings were of no use to him now.

She went towards the little group, thinking to remonstrate with them. As she approached, Jerry said, 'I don't think he is dead. He just moved.'

She dropped her bundle and pushed between the boys, crouching down, her face near the man's head. A faint breath touched her cheek and she put her hand against his neck, feeling a weak

6

pulse fluttering against her fingers.

'You're right, Jerry. He is alive. You must help me get him home.'

'You're joking, Miss,' the boy said.

'I'm not. We can't leave him. He'll drown.'

'But you don't know nothin' about 'im. 'E could be a villain, a murderer even. What you goin' to do with 'im?'

'I'll look after him till he's better and send him home to his family.'

Jerry gave a short laugh. 'You nuts or what?'

Carrie thought she probably was mad. But she couldn't leave the man to drown in the encroaching tide. 'All right, I'll move him myself,' she said, grabbing the inert form by its shoulders and pulling him away from the water's edge.

'Come on then, I'll give you an 'and,' Jerry said. 'Come on lads, you 'eard the lady. Let's get 'im 'ome.'

Unwillingly the boys lifted the body of the stranger and set off across the narrowing strip of mud. Carrie picked up her bundle of coal and wood and followed. It took some effort to get the man up the steps and several of the boys were all for leaving him.

But Jerry chivvied them on and at last the unconscious man was deposited in the handcart the boys had brought along with them.

As they neared Brewers Court the mudlarks melted away into the fog until only Jerry was left. At the door to her house, Carrie turned to him gratefully. 'I wish I could give you something for your help,' she said.

Jerry looked embarrassed. 'It's all right, Miss. We had a good night anyway.' He nodded at the man sprawled on the cart. 'You think 'e's gonna be all right?'

'I hope so. Help me get him inside will you?'

The room struck chill and Carrie tutted with annoyance when she saw that Josiah had let the fire go out. He was slumped in the chair in front of the grate, an empty bottle on the floor by his side, gurgling snores issuing from his open mouth.

'Father, how could you?' she muttered, dumping the pile of fuel in the fireplace. She didn't ask much of him these days, but keeping the fire going in an effort to drive out the damp was simple enough surely.

She was beginning to lose all respect for the man she had loved so unreservedly when she was a child.

She and Jerry carried the still unconscious man inside and deposited him on the threadbare couch which normally served as her father's bed.

Well, he seemed comfortable enough in the chair, Carrie thought, as he gave an extra loud snore, shifted into a more comfortable position and began to breathe more quietly.

Carrie turned up the gas lamp and stood looking down at the man she had helped to rescue from a watery death.

Jerry removed the stranger's boots and jacket.

'We ought to get his breeches off,

too, Miss,' the boy said. 'They're soppin' wet.'

She could see the sense of that and together they managed to peel off the soaking wet garment. She was relieved that Jerry didn't suggest removing the rest of his clothes.

She pulled her shawl from her shoulders and covered the man with it.

'Thank you, Jerry. You've been a big help,' she said, opening the door.

'Good luck, Miss. Let's 'ope 'e don't die on yer,' the boy said with a mischievous grin as he disappeared into the fog.

Carrie went to the sink and poured water into an enamel bowl. Using a corner of her shawl she cleaned the mud from the stranger's face. His skin was dark, weathered, as if he'd spent time in a hot country.

But his hair, when she combed the dried mud out of it, was fair. Maybe he was a sailor, she thought, fallen overboard from a passing ship.

But the jacket and boots were of

good quality, not the clothes of an aristocrat, but they had probably been made by a London tailor.

A merchant doing business along the wharves? Robbed and pushed into the water? It was all too possible, Carrie knew. Since coming to live in this part of London she had soon learnt that there were those desperate enough to kill for a few coins.

The man stirred and opened his eyes. They were of a startling sapphire blue. Carrie noticed, before registering the confusion and terror in his face. He tried to sit up, his eyes darting round the small room, before sinking back on to the cushion.

Carrie lifted a cup to his lips and he drank a little water, then began coughing. She wiped his lips with the corner of the shawl, urging him to rest.

Time enough to question him when he'd had a sleep and regained his strength.

★   ★   ★

As Eliza turned over in bed, she realised she was alone. Where was Carrie? Why hadn't she come to bed? She sat up, listened intently, peering into the darkness. Sounds muffled by the fog came from the nearby highway. But the house was quiet.

Eliza knew her sister often went out at night, but she had yet to summon up the courage to ask where she went. She might be young but she was no longer innocent. Living here these past months had taught her more about life and human nature than she wanted to know, despite Carrie's attempts to shield her.

The truth was she'd put off questioning her because she was afraid of what the answer might be.

Eliza knew she was the one who should feel ashamed. After all, whatever Carrie did, it was for her and their father. She never thought about herself. Ever since their mother had died, Carrie had taken on the burden of caring for her family with never a word of complaint. Even when she'd been offered a position as governess to Lady Arabella Linton's children, she had refused, not wanting to leave her father and sister to fend for themselves.

She could still have been living in Denton Heath, their home village, with her own room and bath at Denton Manor, good food and constant warmth.

But the Martins had been evicted from their home, the factory in the hands of their creditors. Carrie had been offered work, but fourteen-year-old Eliza, pampered and mollycoddled all her young life, had no skills to offer an employer. Josiah Martin, broken by the death of his wife and the loss of his business, was no use in the crisis, taking refuge in drink.

It was up to Carrie to keep the family together until the better times came — times which Carrie constantly assured them were, 'just round the corner'. But those better times were slow in coming. In fact, things had gone from bad to worse.

Eliza shivered, only now fully realising the extent of her sister's sacrifice.

She pulled the blanket round her shoulders and snuggled down into the lumpy mattress, trying to get comfortable. She wished Carrie would come to bed. Snuggled up against her sister, she would not only be warmer, but feel some of the security she had known as a child.

A sob caught in her throat and, to shut out the reality of the present, Eliza indulged in a fantasy where everything was as it had been two years ago. She was at a ball, wearing her first almost grown-up dress, white satin adorned with blue bows.

Her hair was piled high with mother of pearl combs, a few curls allowed to escape and lie on her neck. She knew she looked beautiful, hadn't mother and father told her so? And when Thomas Linton asked her to dance she was in heaven.

Eliza squeezed her eyes shut and

hummed the waltz tune, willing herself to recapture the feel of Thomas's strong arms whirling her round, trying to lose herself in the rapturous memory. But it was no good and the tears trickled through her closed eyelids. She knew in her heart she would never dance again.

The dreadful cough she'd had since her last bout of illness recurred whenever she made the slightest effort leaving her faint and breathless. She turned her face into the pillow to hide her sobs. She didn't want Carrie to know she'd been crying.

At last she fell asleep and when she woke again the room was filled with grey light. Carrie was sleeping beside her, but she stirred and opened her eyes when Eliza sat up. Her face was pale and there were blue shadows around her eyes.

'Are you all right, Carrie?' Eliza asked, her voice filled with alarm, concerned that her sister had fallen prey to the illness she suffered.

'I'm just tired that's all. It's been a

long night.' Carrie swung her legs out of the bed and stood up. 'I must get up, there's a lot to do today.'

'I think I'll come down too. I'm feeling much better today,' Eliza said.

Carrie put her hand to her mouth. 'Before you go down, there's something I must tell you. We have a visitor. He's sleeping on the couch.'

'Carrie, we can't have anyone to stay here. There's no room.' Eliza was horrified. She didn't want anyone from their old life to see how they lived now. And she could not imagine Carrie giving any of their new acquaintances a bed for the night. 'Who is it?' she asked, curiosity getting the better of her.

'I don't know his name, but from his clothes I should say he's from a good family.' Carrie told her how Jerry had helped to bring the unconscious man home. 'I couldn't leave him to drown, could I?'

Eliza's curiosity about the stranger was truly aroused now and she too got out of bed. With frequent pauses to catch her breath, she dressed and washed her face in the bowl of cold water that stood on the rickety nightstand. As she started to comb her hair, a shout from downstairs startled her.

'Who the hell are you — and what are you doing in my house?' That was her father's voice.

'No, no, leave me alone.' She could barely make out the words.

Carrie rushed downstairs and Eliza followed her.

Her father was bending over the stranger, shaking him by the shoulders, while the young man feebly tried to push him away. His face was a mask of terror, his eyes wild and staring.

Eliza stood at the foot of the stairs, her hand over her mouth, her breathing ragged. How could Carrie let this stranger into their home, such as it was? He could be a thief or a murderer for all they knew.

2

It took Carrie some time to explain to her father why she had brought the young man home. He was angry at first. 'We barely have enough to feed ourselves, let alone take care of a stranger,' he said.

'So, I should have left him to drown then?' Carrie demanded.

'Of course not. But you could have called the constable or the river bailiff. I hear they are quite used to fishing corpses out the river,' Josiah said.

'It was the middle of the night, thick fog and no one to call. It seemed the Christian thing to do.'

'Maybe, maybe . . . ' he muttered.

Carrie was relieved that he didn't ask why she'd been abroad at that late hour. But it had been a long time since Father had shown any interest in what his daughters did. He never questioned where the food on the table came from and likewise, Carrie never asked about the source of the booze he consumed. Although he had promised never to do so again, she suspected that he still gambled.

She turned back to the couch where the young man had fallen back against the cushion, muttering feverishly. She called to Eliza to fetch some water and a cloth.

As she bathed his face, she gasped, noticing the livid bruise on his temple for the first time. 'He must have fallen overboard and banged his head,' she said.

As she spoke, his eyes opened and his hands lashed out, knocking her arm away. 'No, no,' he shouted, and lapsed into unconsciousness again.

'He's not going to die, is he?' Eliza asked.

'I don't think so. But he is very ill. I wish we could afford a doctor.'

'What do you think happened to him?'

'If he was on board a ship, he probably fell overboard. Or he could have been robbed and pushed into the river.' She pointed to the heap of damp clothes in the corner of the room. 'I went through his pockets, but there was no wallet or anything to tell us who he might be.'

'He must have been robbed then,' Eliza said.

'We'll find out when he wakes properly,' Carrie said, poking the fire and putting a pan of water over the coals. She stirred some oatmeal into it, all the food they had in the house. 'Now come and eat your breakfast. You must keep your strength up.' She handed her sister a bowl of the thin porridge. 'You too, Father.'

'Aren't you having any?' Eliza asked.

'Later,' Carrie said, pulling up a stool next to the couch and bathing the young man's face again. The livid bruise stood out against his pale skin and she hoped the blow had not harmed him irreparably. His fear and confusion could have been a result of being knocked unconscious, but there could be some underlying cause. She willed him to wake up and tell them what had happened to him.

When he had finished his porridge, Josiah stood up and took his coat off the back of the chair.

'Where are you off to, Father?' Eliza asked.

'I did hear that someone wanted a clerk at one of the warehouses down near the river,' he said. 'I thought I'd go and see whether the position has been filled yet.' He opened the door, letting in a swirl of thick yellow fog.

Eliza took a woollen scarf from the hook behind the door and lovingly wrapped it round his neck. 'Take care,' she said, kissing his cheek. 'And good luck with the job.'

He hesitated. 'Maybe I should stay home today. I don't like the idea of leaving you girls alone in the house with a strange man.'

Carrie looked up from her stool. 'I

hardly think he is in any condition to harm us,' she said. 'Go — before the job is taken.'

'Yes, my dear. You're right, of course.' He went out and Carrie let out a sigh of frustration. Each day Josiah left the house under the pretext of looking for work, but she suspected that he did not try very hard. Yet he always came back smelling the worse for drink, sometimes with a bottle or two hidden inside his coat. Very rarely, he tossed a few coins down on the table or brought back a package of faggots or pies bought from a street vendor.

The Martins' descent into poverty had been gradual. When Josiah had lost the factory, their fine house in Denton Heath had been sold to pay his debts. But there was still some good furniture and the jewellery left by Carrie's mother.

They had taken a small house on the outskirts of Gravesend and, although they had been a lot worse off than before, they had been able to employ a maid and a daily woman. Josiah had found employment in the offices of an importer of fine wines. But, used to running his own business and giving orders, he did not take kindly to being on the receiving end of his employer's sharp tongue. The job lasted less than six months and the maid and daily woman had to go.

They had moved to a small terraced house in south London where Josiah thought it would be easier to find employment. But no job lasted long. Employers soon realised that his frequent absences through so-called illness were really due to over-indulgence in strong drink.

Finally they'd ended up in this miserable court with its standpipe at the entrance, shared earth closet and the attendant smells and dirt. Carrie had never spoken a word in criticism of her father. Her mother's early death from a painful illness, together with the loss of his business, had been too much for Josiah to bear and he had sunk into a deep depression.

Eliza sympathised. She too, was still grieving for her mother. And, being so young, she had not realised that it was Father's own fault that the factory had gone under. But Carrie knew about his gambling and she was getting tired of making excuses for him, of being the one to worry about the rent and food and clothing.

The young man she had rescued tossed and turned feverishly on the couch. What had she been thinking of? He was just one more worry in a life filled with worry. She glanced at her sister who had pulled a chair up to the fire and sat hunched over it, her shawl drawn tightly round her shoulders. Poor Eliza.

Carrie knew that she often day-dreamed about their old life. But she never complained. She had always been frail and their poverty had made an already weak constitution worse. The poor girl was constantly racked with coughs and this foggy weather did not help.

Carrie felt guilty. She should be looking after her sister, not some stranger.

Eliza seemed to sense her sister's gaze and she looked up. 'What are we going to do if Father doesn't get the job?'

'I'm sure he will. But he won't get paid straight away though.'

'We've got no money and no food. Do you think you'll get a reward for rescuing him?' She nodded to the figure on the couch.

'I hadn't thought of such a thing,' Carrie protested. 'Anyway, you needn't worry about money. I still have something to sell. I'll go and get it,' she said, hurrying up the stairs.

She took out the small box containing a silver locket, a gift from her mother on her sixteenth birthday. It was the last thing Mother had given her before her death and Carrie had hoped never to have to part with it. But they had to eat and they couldn't rely on Father.

Biting her lip, she ran downstairs and showed the locket to Eliza.

'No, Carrie, you can't sell that. You mustn't . . . ' She started to cry and Carrie put her arms round her, soothing her when she began to cough again.

'You must have medicine for your cough, dearest,' she said. 'It's no use crying. Just be thankful we still have something to sell. It will see us through until Father is able to provide for us once more.

Eliza dried her tears and smiled. 'You'll be able to buy it back, won't you? When Father is working again?'

'Of course. That's what pawnshops are for. It's like borrowing the money,' Carrie reassured her, putting the little box into her pocket. She didn't add that it would probably cost more to retrieve the locket than they would get for it. Or that it was unlikely she'd ever be in a position to do so.

A crash from the other side of the room distracted them and she rushed to pick up the bowl that the young man had knocked to the floor. He was sitting up, staring round in confusion. 'What am I doing here?' he asked.

Carrie pushed him back against the pillows. 'You had an accident. Just rest for a moment. Then you can tell us what happened.'

'I don't know. I can't remember.' A look of terror crossed his face and he began to breathe quickly. His fingers gripped the blanket that covered him.

'Tell us your name, where you're from.'

'My name? I — I can't remember.'

Carrie sat beside him and took his hand. 'You've had a bang on the head. It's left you a little confused. Just relax and it will come back to you.'

'Am I in hospital? Are you a nurse? You don't look like a nurse,' he said.

'I'm not a nurse. I found you down by the river and brought you home. Don't you remember how you got there, where you were going — anything.'

27

He shook his head frantically. 'I think I was going home.' His eyes closed and he slipped into unconsciousness again, breathing heavily and murmuring as his fingers twisted and kneaded the blanket.

'I think we should leave him to sleep,' Carrie said. 'Maybe he'll be more coherent when he's rested.' She picked up a pail and opened the door. 'I'll get some more water before I go to the pawnshop.'

She filled the bucket at the standpipe and hurried back indoors. It was bitterly cold. She made up the fire and tidied away the breakfast things.

'Now, Eliza, will you be all right with our guest while I'm out? I'll try not to be too long. Just keep the fire going and bathe his face from time to time.'

'I'll be fine, Carrie. As you said, he's harmless enough in that state.'

'And if he wakes, don't badger him with questions. Let him tell us what happened in his own way.' She turned at the door. 'And don't forget — keep the door locked. Don't answer to anyone at all.'

Carrie closed the door behind her, waiting until she heard the bolt shoot home before hurrying out of Brewers Court. She hated leaving her sister alone at any time. She had no fear of the stranger, but there were other dangers lurking for a pretty innocent like Eliza.

The fog had cleared but the day was overcast and grey with a cold wind. Carrie shivered and pulled her shawl closely round her. She saw Jerry leaning against the wall at the entrance to Brewers Court, scuffing his worn shoe against the pavement. In daylight he looked even dirtier than he had the night before and the sores round his mouth looked red and angry.

'How are you this morning, Jerry? None the worse for our little adventure I hope,' Carrie said with a smile.

'I'm aright. What about the toff? 'E didn't die on yer, did 'e?' The boy shivered in his thin clothes and Carrie wished she could do something for him.

'He's quite well, thank you. Had a nasty bang on the head, but he'll live.' Carrie made to walk on, then paused. 'How did you know he was a toff?' she asked.

'Quality boots they was. And soft 'ands. 'E ain't never done a day's work, betcha.' Jerry's eyes gleamed. 'Ere, Miss, you reckon there's a reward for 'im, for us savin' 'is life like?'

'If there is, you'll get your share, Jerry. The thing is, he seems to have lost his memory. Doesn't know who he is at the moment. But I'm sure when he's feeling better he'll be able to tell us.'

'You won't forget that I 'elped yer, will yer, Miss?'

'Of course I won't. He would have drowned without you.'

Jerry grinned and ran off down the road and Carrie turned into the High Street smiling. He wasn't a bad lad and he deserved a reward — if there was one.

Wapping High Street was crowded.

Women in shawls with baskets hooked over their arms jostled with street traders shouting their wares, shops spilled their goods out on to the pavements and everywhere dogs and urchins ducked and dived among the pedestrians and wheeled traffic rumbling over the cobbles.

Carrie threaded her way through the crowd, her hand tightly clasping the precious silver locket. It wouldn't do for it to be stolen before she reached the pawnbroker's.

As she reached an alleyway leading down to the wharves, the crowd parted to allow a group of men to pass. Four of them carried a stretcher, the body it contained barely covered by a hastily flung tarpaulin. Behind them a tall elegantly dressed man was accompanied by a constable. He covered his mouth with a handkerchief and nodded as the constable made a note in his book.

'Another poor geezer claimed by Father Thames,' one bystander remarked.

'Did 'e fall, or was he pushed?' another asked with a cackle of laughter.

Carrie glared at him. Drownings were commonplace along the river, almost every tide washed up a drunk who had taken a wrong turning, a victim of robbery or a suicide. But there was no need to make a joke of it.

The well-dressed man brushed past her. As he turned to apologise she looked up into eyes of an intense blue. He did not smile, merely touched his hat and walked on behind the men with their gruesome burden.

Carrie stared after him, wondering where she had seen him before. He seemed out of place in this part of London, although she knew that some of the *toffs* as Jerry called them, came to the East End in search of adventure. They called it slumming, but they usually frequented the pubs and music halls at night.

She dismissed the thought, hurrying up Wapping Lane towards the pawnbroker's, wondering how much the old skinflint would offer for the locket. Not as much as it was worth, that was sure. But Carrie was learning the art of haggling. It was amazing how hunger and deprivation sharpened the wits.

The pawnbroker held the silver locket up to the light, pulling a face and shaking his head. 'Can't give you much on that,' he said. 'Not worth a lot — now if it was gold, my dear . . . '

'I know silver's not worth as much, but it was an expensive item. My mother paid a lot for it,' Carrie protested.

'Your mother, you say. Now why would you be hocking something your mother gave you?'

Carrie held out her hand. 'If you won't give me a fair price, I'll go elsewhere.'

The pawnbroker snatched the locket out of her reach. 'Well, if it was your mother's and you've fallen on hard times, I might reconsider. Only you see, it might be stolen. I have to consider that.'

'I'm not a thief,' Carrie said indignantly.

The little man put his head on one side, smiling faintly. 'I think I believe you, missie. Still, five shillin' only — that's all I can allow you.'

Carrie knew the locket had cost several pounds, but she was in no position to argue. If she shopped carefully, five shillings would keep them in food for some time and there would even be enough to buy some cough medicine for Eliza. She nodded agreement before the pawnbroker could change his mind and scurried out of the shop with the coins clutched in her hand.

Turning a corner, she cannoned into someone and, looking up to apologise, found herself staring into the same blue eyes she had encountered earlier. The man put out a hand to steady her, grasping her wrist.

'We meet again,' he said, his lip curling in a smile that held no warmth.

Carrie fought the urge to pull away. 'I'm sorry, sir. I did not see you in my haste,' she said.

'No harm done,' he replied, still holding on to her wrist. 'And where might a pretty thing like you be dashing off to?'

She did not reply and he looked up and down insolently, taking in her old and worn, but good quality dress. 'You don't seem to be the usual drab found around these parts. A lady fallen on hard times I wager? He raised an eyebrow.

'I'm a respectable girl from a respectable family. That's all you need to know. And now, sir, if you will let go my arm, I will be about my business.' Carrie did not like the way he was looking at her and she felt a chill of apprehension as his eyes raked her figure once more. But she stared boldly at him. She wouldn't let him see she was afraid.

He laughed and let her go. 'No matter. My business often brings me to these parts. I am sure we will meet again.' He strolled off with a swagger and she stood watching until he was out of sight, rubbing her wrist and wishing she had kicked him in the shins.

3

When she reached home, her arms laden with purchases, Carrie was pleased to see that for the first time in weeks, Eliza had colour in her cheeks, the old sparkle back in her eyes. Looking after their impromptu guest had given her something to think about besides their depressing situation.

The young man was still semi-conscious, muttering from time to time. When Carrie leaned over him to feel his forehead, he began shouting incoherently, trying to fight her off. Despite her reassurances, he did not quieten until she walked away.

'I think it best we leave him,' she whispered to Eliza. 'He's not quite so feverish now. I think the trouble is more in his mind than his body.'

'Do you mean he is mad? Could he have escaped from an asylum?' Eliza's eyes widened and she put a hand to her mouth.

'Not mad, silly — just confused. He seems afraid of something — or somebody.' Carrie put the provisions in the cupboard under the dresser and began to prepare the vegetables she'd bought in the market. With the shin bone she'd got from the butcher she would make a nourishing thick broth that would do both Eliza and the stranger good.

'I had thought of trying to find out something about our guest,' she said. 'Maybe someone knows who he is. But if he was attacked as I suspect, the culprit may wish to do him more harm. I think we should keep his presence here quiet until we know more about him.'

Eliza glanced towards the couch where the young man now appeared to be sleeping naturally. 'He kept shouting and mumbling while you were out,' she said.

'What was he saying?'

'I couldn't make it out. He kept

shouting 'No' and something about being too late. But it didn't really make sense.'

'I hope he comes to his senses soon. If not, we should try to get him to the Infirmary. The nuns will be better placed to look after him,' Carrie said.

The broth simmered in its pot over the fire and the girls toasted their toes while they waited for it to cook. The firelight shone on dark and fair heads as they whispered together so as not to disturb the sleeping invalid. It was a homely scene that belied the poverty of the starkly-furnished room

The cosy atmosphere was shattered when the door flew open and their father stumbled in, bringing with him a blast of icy air. One look at his face told them that the promised employment had not materialised. But somewhere he had found the money to buy a bottle. It hung half-empty from his hand as he stood glaring round him, defying them to comment on his condition.

Eliza had been snuggled down in his armchair, the only comfortable one in the room. She leapt up and offered it to him, tried to help him off with his coat. But he pushed her aside and fell into the chair with a grunt, closing his eyes and raising the bottle to his mouth.

Tight-lipped, Carrie snatched it from him and put it on the dresser. 'Dinner will be ready soon, Father,' she said, her voice cold.

He glanced towards the couch. 'I see our guest is still here,' he said. 'How long must I give up my bed for him?'

'You shall have your bed tonight, Father,' Carrie reassured him. 'The young man will surely be on his way when he is rested.'

Josiah grunted and said no more. Carrie served his bowl of broth and he tucked into it hungrily, not moving from his place by the fire. She and Eliza ate theirs at the table.

When they had finished, she tried to feed some of the broth to the stranger. He coughed and spluttered, but some of it seemed to go down. After a few moments he feebly pushed her hand away, but she was relieved to see more colour in his cheeks and the bruise on his temple was a little less vivid.

She gently covered him with the blanket and in minutes he was sleeping peacefully. Their father too was sleeping in the armchair, having retrieved his bottle from the dresser. Soon, his drunken snores reverberated round the small room.

Carrie fetched her sewing from the cupboard under the dresser and she and her sister worked quietly together, occasionally casting anxious glances at the young man asleep on the couch. In a silence only broken by Josiah's snores and the crackle of the fire, Carrie could almost imagine that nothing had changed in her life.

A log settled in the hearth, sending up a shower of sparks, and Carrie's eyes opened to the reality of the present. No dainty embroidery now, but the workmanlike needlework of make do and mend. In the past two years, Carrie had learned to be practical.

On her rare excursion to the better part of the city, she had seen that fashions were changing. The large unwieldy crinolines with their yards of superfluous material had given way to a sleeker look. Of course, Carrie and her sister had abandoned the wire hoops that held their skirts away from their bodies long ago. Apart from not wishing to look out of place in these new surroundings, they would never have got through the narrow entrance to Brewers Court.

But the voluminous skirts had proved a boom for the sisters. They had managed to cut them down and make two skirts out of one. Now Carrie was working on another of her old dresses, one she had been reluctant to sell, hoping the day would come when she would have the opportunity to wear fine clothes once more. Those times were unlikely now, she acknowledged and she had persuaded Eliza that they could re-style their old dresses in the new fashion and sell them as new.

'They will fetch a higher price. That old woman in the market only pays pennies for second-hand clothes,' she told Eliza.

Tonight they were working on a dress of rich blue silk, the one Carrie had worn to their last ball when Eliza had danced with Thomas Linton.

As she carefully undid the stitches which joined the skirt to the bodice, Eliza sighed. 'Your beautiful dress, Carrie. You looked so lovely in it — like a princess.'

'I'll have lovely dresses again one day, never fear — and so will you,' Carrie replied, forcing a smile. She knew her sister was dreading the day that she'd have to surrender her own ball dress to the scissors — and with it her daydreams of dancing once more with the heir to Denton Manor.

They worked on in silence until their father woke with a start, demanding in a harsh voice where the damned maid had got with their tea.

Stanley Travers stood in the mortuary in the basement of the Infirmary looking down at the body on the table. He appeared grief-stricken, but he was unmoved by the gruesome sight of the drowned man.

He'd known the moment they pulled the corpse from the water that it was not his cousin, despite the pallor of death, it was evident his face and body had been tanned a dark mahogany from working outdoors.

But Adam had been abroad for several years and his skin could have browned and coarsened from the hot sun of the West Indies. It was a mistake anyone could make, Stanley thought, covering his face with a handkerchief to hide his smile of satisfaction. He was apprehensive too. Was Adam really dead? He had to be. But Stanley couldn't rely on the real body turning up later. There was no time.

He had to prove to old Justin

Rosebury that his grandson was dead. And nothing but a body would suffice. He would return to Canterbury tomorrow. If a second body turned up later, it could remain unidentified and be consigned to a pauper's grave. Thank God this man carried no possession to identify him.

He put a hand to his pocket where Adam's wallet and gold signet ring lay. The men he had hired had handed them over as proof that the deed was done and he had paid them well.

They assured him there was nothing left on the body to lead to his identity and, although he did not believe them, there was nothing he could do about it now. If Adam still possessed the gold watch he'd been given on this twenty-first birthday, the thugs had probably stolen it, regarding it as extra payment.

Stanley smiled. If they got caught trying to sell such a valuable object, it would lend credence to the story that Adam had been set on by thieves and thrown in the river.

He started as the constable touched his arm and coughed. 'I'm sorry you had to go through this, Sir,' he said. 'If you'd just sign this form, stating that the body is that of your cousin, Adam Rosebury, we'll release it to you for burial.'

'Yes, I must take him home.' Stanley put the handkerchief up to his eyes. 'My poor grandfather, he will be profoundly shocked . . . ' He turned away as if to hide his grief.

'Might I suggest, Sir, a closed coffin would be best. I feel it would be too distressing for the family to see him like this — so young too. Still, the wharves and quaysides are treacherous at night.'

'We were looking forward to his homecoming. He'd been working abroad, you see. I knew his ship would dock this week and I wanted to welcome him home. I put up at an inn, the *Prospect of Whitby*, near here — waiting for news of his ship.'

'What made you think this might be your cousin?' the constable asked.

'I learned the ship had docked, but when I inquired, I was told he'd already come ashore. He was supposed to meet me at the inn but he didn't turn up. I was on my way to make inquiries this morning when I heard . . . ' Stanley faltered, as if overcome with grief once more. 'I never dreamed it could really be Adam . . . '

The constable nodded sympathetically. 'These tragedies are all too common when fog sweeps up from the sea,' he said. 'At least you know what happened to him. Some are never recovered when the tide is running strong.'

After receiving directions to the undertaker's, Stanley took his leave, confident that he would hear no more of the matter. Once arrangements had been made for the transfer of his so-called cousin's body to the family home in Lower Chilton a few miles from Canterbury, Stanley's thoughts turned to amusing himself for the evening. A night spent with a willing doxie would be preferable to a lonely bed at the *Prospect of Whitby*.

A picture rose in his mind of the girl he had bumped into that morning, chestnut curls and brown eyes, tall and slim, a little too slim for his liking. He preferred a more buxom wench. But she had spirit — he liked that. He chuckled, remembering how she had seen him off when he had sought to detain her.

He pushed his way along the crowded street and into a dingy public house. It was packed with stevedores and sailors and he wrinkled his nose fastidiously at the smell of unwashed humanity in so small a space.

Ignoring oaths and curses, he fought his way to the bar and beckoned the barman who was swabbing the counter with a dirty cloth.

'Is Alf about?' he asked.

'Who wants 'im?'

'That's my business. Where he is?'

The barman jerked his head. 'In the back,' he said.

Stanley pushed open the door at the

end of the bar and went down two steps into a dingy back room where Alf was sprawled in a high-backed chair, his legs stretched out towards the fire. A girl was perched on his lap, her fingers stroking his beard.

When Stanley entered, Alf pushed the girl away and pointed to the door. 'Business, me girl, out you go.'

The girl pouted and turned to smile at Stanley. But he ignored her, waiting till the door closed before pulling up a chair before the fire.

'My business keeps me here another day and I have a mind for company tonight,' he said.

Stanley became impatient.

'I met a girl today, coming out of the pawnshop on the corner of Brewhouse Lane. Tall, dark hair, brown eyes — you wouldn't happen to know her by any chance?'

'A doxie, was she?'

'No, no. Very refined — not the usual sort you see round these parts,' Stanley said.

'Fancy 'er, do you?'

'Not at all. I thought I knew her and wondered what she was doing in Wapping. I thought she might be in need of help,' Stanley lied.

'I'll keep me eyes open for yer,' Alf promised.

When he'd gone, Alf supped his beer thoughtfully, sure that Carrie was the girl Travers had described. But he had plans for her himself — and for her sister.

Ever since the Martin girls had moved into Brewers Court he'd seen their potential. Girls like them, down on their luck, always resisted the most obvious way to make a living, preferring to starve rather than losing their so-called respectability. But when starvation and eviction from their lodgings threatened, the time would be right to make his move.

The older one, Carrie, would be hardest to break but he knew she'd do anything to protect her sister.

4

Carrie was becoming concerned about their guest despite the fact that each day he seemed to grow stronger physically. He had been with them for a week now, the bruises were starting to fade and he was able to get up for a while during the day, although he never ventured out of the house unless it was to cross the yard to the privy.

The young man, who they had decided to call Mr Jones, had politely but firmly, given up the couch to Josiah and now slept on a makeshift bed on the floor, but although he seemed physically fit, Carrie still wondered about his mental state. He spent hours gazing into the fire, his face screwed up as if trying to remember his past. And too often that look of terror would come into his eyes and he would cry out.

What could have happened to frighten him so?' Eliza whispered one evening as they sat at their sewing. *Mr Jones* had been twitching in his sleep again.

'He looks as if he was quite fit and strong before the accident or whatever it was,' Carrie replied. 'He probably was attacked and robbed, but he doesn't seem the sort to be frightened of a couple of thugs. More likely he tried to fight them off.'

'But the blow on his head made him lose his memory?'

'Possible, but I think there's more behind it.' Carrie glanced at the young man. She and Eliza had spent many hours trying to puzzle out their guest's story. Some of the explanations her younger sister had put forward bordered on fantasy and she couldn't help smiling. It had certainly served to divert Eliza from the boredom of sewing the long seams on the skirts they were making.

But they needed the money. Their

father was seldom at home now and when he did return there was no mention of work. And yet he was always the worse for the drink so he must be getting money from somewhere, although none of it found its way into their household budget. The little money Carrie had got from the pawnbroker for her silver locket had almost gone and they had nothing left to sell.

Carrie paused in her sewing. 'Eliza, dear, I shall have to go out tonight. You will be alright with Mr Jones, won't you?'

'Of course. But you said we can sell the skirts. Is it really necessary for you to carry on mudlarking as you call it?'

'I'm afraid it is, dear. We have very little fuel for the fire and it grows colder each day. I worry about your cough returning. You've been so much better since I managed to get the medicine for you.' Carrie laid a hand over her sister's. 'I'll try not to be too long.'

'You won't bring back another lodger

will you?' Eliza said with a mischievous smile.

'I'll try not to.' She glanced across at Mr Jones. 'He can't stay here forever but I don't know what to do about him.'

'We should have sent him to the Infirmary,' Eliza said.

'I think the way he was raving, not knowing who he was, the poor man would have ended up in the asylum,' Carrie said. 'I hate the thought of that.' The truth was, that although she knew Mr Jones would have to leave them soon, she didn't want him to go. She told herself it was because he had been so good for Eliza. Helping to look after their unexpected guest had taken her mind off their troubles. Her listlessness had gone, replaced by a little of her old sparkle. The change was not entirely due to the medicine Carrie had managed to buy.

She stood up and took her shawl off the nail on the back of the door, pausing to look down at the sleeping man. His head turned restlessly and his eyelids twitched as if he was in the grip of a nightmare. Without thinking, Carrie stretched out a hand to brush the hair back from his forehead. At her touch, his eyes flew open and his hands came up to ward her off. She thought he was going to strike her, as he had several times during his delirium. But this time, his hand grasped hers and he smiled at her, his blue eyes clear and steady in his tanned face.

'I know what you've done for me and I can't thank you enough, Miss Martin,' he said. 'I won't trespass on your hospitality much longer. I have no wish to be a burden to you.'

Her heart was beating fast and she felt a flush creeping up her face. She was conscious of the warmth of her hand in his and for a moment she had the foolish thought that she would be happy if he carried on holding it forever.

'I assure you, you are not a burden, Mr Jones,' Carrie said, hoping her voice did not betray her feelings. 'Please don't feel you have to leave until you are completely well.' With an effort, she pulled her hand away and settled her shawl on her shoulders. 'I have to go out. My sister will get you some broth. We'll talk when I get back.'

Outside, Carrie leaned against the wall to catch her breath, giving herself a mental shake. She was being as silly as Eliza with her foolish daydreams of Thomas Linton.

She crossed Brewers Court and hurried through the alley towards the main road. A thin sleety rain fell, creating misty haloes round the gas lamps and she did not notice the figure lurking in the shadows until he moved into the light. She hurried forward, thinking it was Jerry. He often accompanied her on her *mudlarking* expeditions now, showing her the places where the richest pickings could be found.

'Good evening, Miss. What are you doing out on a night like this?'

It was Alf Budgen who lived next door to the Martins. Carrie muttered a brief 'good evening'. She didn't like the man and tried to avoid him, despite her upbringing, she didn't care that he and Nancy lived together as husband and wife. But she hated him for allowing Nancy to earn her living as she did.

He grasped her wrist as she tried to walk past. 'I know what you're up to, girl,' he said, pushing his face close to hers so that she could smell the whisky and tobacco on his breath.

She recoiled, but managed to answer. 'I don't know what you mean.'

'You're trying to take the bread out of my Nancy's mouth, that's what.' He gave her a little shake. 'And I'm not 'avin' it, see. If you wants to go on the game, you sees me about it. I say where you touts fer trade, get me?'

It took a minute for Carrie to understand what he was implying and she almost laughed. 'I can assure you, Mr Budgen, you are wrong. And you have no business talking to me like this.'

She pulled her hand away and rubbed her wrist.

'What else would a so-called respectable girl be doing out at night then?' His voice held a suggestive leer. 'And what about that bloke I've seen at your place? I saw 'im sneakin' out just before daylight . . . '

Carrie gasped. She had hoped no-one was aware of their guest, worried for his safety as much as for her own reputation. Alf must have seen Mr Jones on his way to the privy — that was the only time he had left the house. Thinking quickly she said, 'Mr Budgen — not that it's any of your business who visits me in my home. The person you saw was my cousin. He's visiting us from the country for a few days.'

With that she hurried away into the dark sleety night. She did not question the instinct that had made her lie. Whatever Mr Jones's past might be, she was sure something had happened to make him lose his memory. His terror was no sham. And if someone truly meant to harm him, it was best that as few people as possible knew that he had survived the attack on him.

Carrie was sure that someone had beaten him and left him for dead — it was no ordinary robbery. And Alf Budgen was the sort of man who would sell his knowledge to the highest bidder. She would never forgive herself if she was the cause of any harm coming to Mr Jones.

Lost in thought, she was not aware of footsteps behind her until they were close and she whirled in alarm, thinking Alf Budgen had followed her. But it was Jerry, accompanied by one of his younger brothers.

'You should've waited fer me, Miss. These streets is no place fer a lady,' he panted, wiping his nose on the sleeve of his jacket.

'Thank you for your concern, Jerry. To be truthful I could do with your company. I do get a bit nervous in the dark.' Carrie smiled down at him. Since the night he'd helped her with Mr

Jones, he seemed to have appointed himself her protector. He might live in a hovel and his upbringing left a lot to be desired, but he was more of a gentleman than many she had encountered in her old life.

He held his brother's hand and offered his other arm to Carrie as they crossed the road to the embankment. The tide was out, leaving an expanse of mud pitted by sharp needles of rain. The moon showed through the ragged clouds and there was no need of the rag torches tonight. The tideline was heaped with flotsam and jetsam which gave off a foul stench as Jerry and his brother began turning it over.

The first time she'd done it, Carrie had been sickened by the smell, but now she had learned to breathe shallowly through her mouth and it was almost bearable. Their pickings were slim tonight, but Jerry's brother gave a crow of triumph when he found a leather boot tangled in the seaweed.

His face fell when Jerry said, 'One's

no good, Billy. Yer'll 'ave ter find the other.'

A few minutes later Carrie unearthed its mate. She was pleased but her pleasure was tempered by the thought that the boots' owner might also be lying tangled among the debris at the water line and she suddenly had no stomach for further searching. She gave the boot to Jerry.

She had already gathered a good supply of fuel. That would do for now. She slipped and almost fell, recoiling as her hands sank into the ooze and touched something hard. She picked it up, gasping as a moonbeam touched the object.

Her first thought was to wonder who had lost the ornate gold pocket watch, followed quickly by the shameful realisation that it was obviously valuable and would fetch a good sum at the pawnbroker's on the corner of Brewhouse Lane. It would keep them in food and fuel for a long time. She might even manage to get a doctor for Eliza.

At one time it would never have entered her head to sell something which did not belong to her, but times had changed and Carrie was at last learning to harden her heart against the instincts of her earlier upbringing. Now, her only thought was survival, for her and her family.

She rubbed the watch on her skirt to get rid of the mud and tucked it into her bodice, first glancing round to make sure no-one was watching.

When they reached Brewers Court, Jerry offered to share the proceeds from the sale of the boots, but Carrie declined. His family were in far worse straits than hers. Besides, she thought guiltily, I have the watch. 'Call it payment for your help the other night,' she said.

'How is the gent? Still with yer?' Jerry asked.

'He's much better and talking of leaving,' she said.

As he opened the door to the house opposite, Carrie stopped him. 'The young man we rescued — he's lost his memory. Doesn't know who he is or where he came from. Would you keep your ears open in case someone's asking for him?'

'Yeah. Course I will.' His eyes gleamed and Carrie remembered him speaking of a reward on the night they'd found Mr Jones. Something made her caution him. 'Jerry, promise me. If you hear anything, don't say a word. Come to me immediately.'

He nodded doubtfully and hastened to reassure him. 'Don't worry — if there's a reward, I'll see that you get it, and, Jerry, if anyone asks you, the man staying with us is my cousin, Mr Jones from Kent. Can you remember that?'

'I don't see what's the mystery, but yeah — all right.' He and his brother went indoors and Carrie entered her own home.

The room was lit only by the dying fire. There was no sign of her father and *Mr Jones* appeared to be asleep in his makeshift bed. Eliza must have retired for the night too. Carrie piled the fuel she had gathered beside the hearth and hung up her shawl.

Upstairs she took the watch from her bodice and examined it in the subdued light of the gap lamp at the end of the court. She hadn't looked as it properly until now, although from the brief glimpse she'd had it looked like gold. She rubbed at the encrusted mud and saw that she was right — a gentleman's gold pocket watch. She turned it over, wondering how it had come to be lost. Peering at the intricately entwined initials engraved on the back, she made out an *A* and what looked like a *B* or an *R*.

It must be worth a lot of money and Carrie felt sure it would keep them in food and warmth for the best part of the winter if they were careful. She would ask Nancy where she could get the best price for it. She didn't entirely trust the pawnbroker in Brewhouse Lane where she had sold jewellery before.

But she couldn't sell it. those initials and the unique design meant it would be easily traceable. If the owner saw it in a pawnshop or jewellers, of if he had offered a reward for its recovery, Carrie would be arrested as a thief. And what would happen to her family then? Besides, it was not hers to sell. She might be poor, but she was still honest. She had not sunk so low yet. Better to make inquiries and try to trace the owner herself, she thought, quickly thrusting the watch back into the drawer and slipping into the bed beside her sister.

Lying in the dark she went over Alf Budgen's insinuations. Did he believe that *Mr Jones* was her cousin? Nevertheless, she realised that, if she was to keep her reputation intact, the young man downstairs would have to leave. Now that he was physically fit, she had no excuse for keeping him here.

Her last thought before she fell asleep was that, living the way they did now, her reputation was the last thing she should be worrying about. But, if *Mr Jones* by some miracle returned the feelings she was beginning to have for him, then her reputation was very important indeed.

5

Things were a little easier for the Martins now that *Mr Jones* had managed to find work in one of the warehouses, although Carrie had been appalled that someone who was so obviously a gentleman had fallen to doing such menial work.

But as he said when she protested, 'How do you know I am a gentleman — I do not know myself who I am.' He laughed. 'Whatever my past may be, I have a feeling this sort of work is not new to me. Heaving those sacks of grain on to the wharves seemed to come naturally.' He leaned forward and took her hand. 'I have trespassed on your hospitality for far too long. It's time I began to pay my way, though I would be grateful if you will allow me to stay a little longer.'

'Of course. I only wish the accommodation were more suitable,' she said.

She hesitated, blushing a little. 'I have told people you are my cousin, visiting from Kent. I hope you do not mind.'

He laughed again. 'I am honoured to be included in your family,' he said.

Eliza came downstairs at that moment and Carrie stood up, conscious that Mr Jones was still holding on to her hand. She hurried forward and took the bundle of clothing from her sister, hoping her blushes were unnoticed.

They began to sort the clothes, deciding what could be re-used in adapting the old-fashioned crinoline dresses to a more modern style. They had begun to build up quite a clientele among Nancy and her friends who all wanted their old skirts re-modelled in the new fashion. Carrie no longer cared what these girls did for a living and besides, she was not too proud to take their money if it meant keeping a roof over their heads.

It was still hard to make ends meet though, especially as Josiah now made no pretence of seeking work. If it had not been for Mr Jones's contribution, there would have been times when Carrie would have been unable to pay the rent. But that wasn't the only reason she welcomed his inclusion in the household.

As she sat by the fire with her sister industriously sewing, she encouraged their guest to talk, hoping something would spark off a memory in his confused mind. And, as they talked, she discovered that they had much in common. He was well-educated and could talk knowledgeably about books, art and music. He could remember everything he'd read and recall concerts he had attended in the past. Only his private life remained a mystery.

One evening, while the rain beat on the windows and sudden gusts of wind sent smoke from the fire swirling into the room, Mr Jones recalled a concert he had attended in the newly-opened Albert Hall which had been named in honour of the Queen's late husband.

'That was before I went to Jamaica,'

he said. 'I was out there for three years . . . '

He hesitated and Carrie looked up sharply. 'What were you doing in Jamaica?' she asked.

He looked confused. 'I don't know. I only know that I have been there at some time in the past.' His hands twisted in his lap and the haunted look came into his eyes again. 'I suppose I must have had some business there.'

Carrie reached across and touched his hand. 'Don't worry about it. I'm sure the memories will return if you don't try to force them. Each day pieces come back. After all, you had not spoken of Jamaica before. Although you knew you had been abroad, you did not recall where.' She smiled and went on with her sewing. 'Tell us about the music you heard at the concert.'

Eliza sighed. 'I wish we could go to the Albert Hall. It is so long since we had any sort of entertainment.'

'You could sing to us,' Carrie said. She turned to Mr Jones. 'My sister has such a sweet singing voice.'

'That was before I developed this cough,' Eliza said. 'Besides I cannot sing unaccompanied. She sighed again. 'I do miss my piano,' she said wistfully.

'My sister used to play and sing too. We had many happy hours . . . ' Mr Jones had spoken and Carrie gasped at the import of what he had said.

'You have a sister? What's her name? Where does she live?' The questions tumbled out before she had time to think.

But he covered his face with his hands and groaned. 'I don't know. It was just a fleeting impression. If only I could remember.'

'I'm sorry. I should not have questioned you,' Carrie said, annoyed with herself. Continuous questioning only confused him and made it even harder to recall anything. But this was the first real clue they'd had to his previous life.

Each day Mr Jones, or *Cousin John* as they were now calling him at his request, regained a little of his memory, although he still had no idea how he had come to be lying face down in the mud at the edge of the River Thames.

'Perhaps you fell overboard from a passing ship,' Carrie suggested a few days later when they were once more going over the few memories Mr Jones had recovered.

'I could make some inquiries about ships that were in the river at the time,' John said. 'I am down by the docks every day and there are always sailors hanging about on the wharves and in the pubs.'

But Carrie noticed a shadow pass across the young man's face and she knew he was thinking it had been no accident.

'Do not put yourself in any danger,' she begged. 'If you should unwittingly approach one of your attackers . . . '

'That is why I have not spoken to anyone before,' John answered. 'I keep to myself, get on with my work. But always I am on the lookout for a face I recognise — whether friend or foe.'

Carrie put a hand on his arm. 'I am sure that your memory will return soon. Why, each day some small thing comes to light.' She pasted a cheerful smile on her face and got up to place more fuel on the fire. As she poked at the glowing coals, she laughed and attempted a joke. 'But I hope it does not return before the winter's end. You see, *Cousin John*, when your memory does return, you will leave us — and what shall we do then for money for coals?'

He laughed too. 'Maybe I am truly a rich merchant or heir to a fortune. If that is so I can assure you, Miss Martin, you and your family will never want for coals or anything else for that matter.'

Carrie tried to tell herself that the warmth on her cheeks was from the fire, but she refrained from turning round until the blush had died down. She really wanted him to get better, of course she did. She would not wish anyone to be forced to live the life they did. But she dreaded the day he must

73

go out of her life forever.

From time to time she dared to hope that he felt the same way. Several times he seemed about to speak and then that familiar shadow would cross his face and he would retreat into silence. Then she would tell herself she was being foolish. She knew nothing about him — he could be a married man with a family for all anyone knew.

But her childish dreams served to take her mind off their dire situation and the growing acceptance that this was to be their lot from now on. Her father would not miraculously come to his senses and begin to provide for his family again, Eliza would never have her piano and *John Jones* would regain his memory and leave them. Meanwhile she would make the most of his company and enjoy the small benefits his contribution to the household brought them.

Eliza began to cough, rousing Carrie from her reverie. Rushing to get the medicine for her sister and helping her upstairs to bed broke the small moments of intimacy, the shared laughter.

Despite the linctus which Carrie had obtained from a nearby apothecary and the fact that the house was no longer quite so cold and damp, Eliza's cough heralded a bout of illness which lasted almost until spring.

During those months Carrie nursed her sister devotedly in between her trips to the market for cheap food and delivering her dress-making endeavours to the neighbours. The rest of the time she sat at her sister's bedside, bathing her forehead and feeding her broth.

The bad weather continued and there were storms at sea which prevented the ships from leaving the Port of London for days at a time. On several occasions John had no work. To add to their misery, there was less sewing for Carrie now that Nancy's friends had all had their dresses altered.

As their fortunes declined once more, Carrie's thoughts often turned to the gold watch, still nestling snugly in the bottom drawer. Her conscience waned a little as she watched Eliza struggling for breath and she thought of the medicine she could buy with the money it would fetch. She would even be able to get a doctor for her beloved sister.

After a night of sitting up once more nursing Eliza, Carrie opened the drawer and took the watch from its hiding place. She held it up to the meagre light from the small window, trying once more to decipher the engraved letters on the back. She told herself that when times were better she would be able to redeem it from the pawnbroker — it wasn't stealing. She would only be borrowing the money.

Then, with a sigh, she wrapped it in a tattered petticoat and put it back in the drawer. It was not hers to sell or to pawn — besides, who would buy a watch with someone else's name engraved on it?

Carrie paced the room in despair. Eliza seemed to be sleeping peacefully at last. But when she woke, the coughing would start again and this time there would be no linctus to soothe her. She could not sell the watch and if John did not find work today she did not know what they would do. If only there was something she could do. And where was Father? He had not been home for two days but she was beginning not to care.

For the first time she could not make excuses for him. His grief at the loss of his wife had hastened his decline, but Mother had been dead nearly three years now. Wasn't it time he started thinking of the living?

Voices in the court outside the window arrested her pacing. She heard Nancy's voice, high indignant.

'I ain't gonna do it — and that's that,' she said.

'You'll do as I say, me girl, if you know which side yer bread's buttered,' Alf shouted.

'You can't make me,' Nancy shouted.

'Oh no?' The threat was followed by

the sound of a blow.

Shouts and curses were common-place in Brewers Court and usually, Carrie tried to ignore it, but this time she threw the door open and confronted her neighbours. She knew better than to berate Alf for his treatment of Nancy. Such men thought it was their right to beat their women. He might even attack her if she interfered. Instead she spoke reasonably, politely requesting them to lower their voices in deference to her sick sister.

'I'm sorry, love. We got a bit carried away,' Nancy said, shooting a defiant look at Alf.

He had the grace to look slightly ashamed but he still kept his grip on Nancy's arm. Carrie noticed that her friend's sleeve was torn and, thinking quickly, she said, 'I'll mend that for you. It won't take a minute. You want to look your best when you go out tonight, don't you?'

Nancy pulled her arm away from Alf

and followed her inside.

Carrie sat her down and fetched a cloth to bathe the bruise that was swelling on Nancy's cheek. 'Why do you stay with him when he treats you so?' she asked.

'Got nowhere else to go, 'ave I?' Nancy shrugged. 'Besides, it's me own fault. He don't like it when I stand up for meself.'

'How can it be your fault?' Carrie asked, getting needle and thread and beginning to repair the sleeve.

'You don't understand.'

'No — I don't. And I don't suppose I ever will.'

'He ain't all bad,' Nancy said. 'I owe him a lot. I'd be in the gutter now if it weren't fer my Alf.'

Carrie thought that the life her friend led was as bad if not worse than being in the gutter as she put it. But, when things were at their worst, hadn't she been tempted to do the same thing for the sake of her sister? She gave an inward shudder.

Yet, would that be any worse than selling something which did not belong to her as she had so recently contemplated?

She finished mending the tear and cut the thread. 'There — it hardly shows,' she said.

'Thanks, love, you're a pal.' Nancy glanced round the shabby ill-furnished room. 'Looks like you're worse off than me,' she said. 'I thought your fancy man was keeping you now.'

It took a moment for Carrie to realise what the other girl meant. 'If you're talking about Mr Jones — I keep telling you, he's my cousin.' But she knew the blush flooding her cheeks had betrayed her.

Nancy laughed. 'If you say so, love. Still, I envy you — wish I could find a nice gentleman to look after me.'

'He's hardly doing that as you can see,' Carrie said. 'When he's in work, he pays his way. We help each other,' she said. 'He needs a place to stay and I need to keep up with the rent.'

Nancy's laugh rang out again. 'Your secret's safe with me, Carrie, love.' She stood up. 'Well, must be going. Thanks for mending me frock.'

'Will you be all right, Nancy?'

'Course I will.' She touched her bruised cheek. 'Alf will've calmed down by now.'

'Why did he hit you? What were you arguing about?'

'Nothing much.'

Carrie could not agree. 'You should leave him,' she said.

'I told you, he's good to me most of the time. Anyway, I can't leave him now. He's got a new business and he's promised me a part of it. I won't have to go on the streets no more.'

It must be something criminal, knowing Alf, Carrie thought. But what could she do about it?

Alf was waiting outside when Nancy left. 'Well, did you ask her?' Carrie heard him say.

'No, I didn't. Ask her yourself,' Nancy said.

Carrie tensed herself for the sound of another blow, but all she heard was the slam of a door, followed by their murmured voices came through the thin walls.

As she prepared the vegetable broth for their dinner she tried to make sense of what she'd heard. They had been talking about her, she was sure. She remembered Nancy teasing her about becoming one of Alf's *girls*. That must be it, she thought. If he was taking Nancy off the streets, he would want another girl to take her place. But she hadn't sunk so low yet.

Once more she said a prayer of thanks for the presence of *Cousin John*. Having a man in the house was some protection from the Alf Budgens of this world.

6

Stanley Towers was becoming impatient. He tried to hide his frustration as he paced the long drawing-room where Sir Justin Rosebury sat in his high-backed wing chair. Tears streamed down the old man's face and he asked the question he had asked so many times over the last few months.

'Are you sure it was Adam — really sure?'

'Grandfather, of course I am. It was Adam — no question of it.'

'I can't believe it, he was coming home. If only I had written sooner . . .' The old man's voice trailed away and he wiped a shaky hand over his face.

The door opened and a girl entered carrying a sheaf of early spring daffodils from the garden. She was about seventeen, slim with fair hair and blue eyes. Insipid, Stanley thought

— not to his taste at all.

He eyed his cousin, Emily, sourly as she put the flowers down and ran to the old man's side. 'Grandfather, do not distress yourself.' She turned to him. 'Have you been badgering him? Can't you see he's not well?'

'He's on about Adam again — can't convince himself the lad's really dead. But I saw the body. It was him,' he said.

'He blames himself,' she said softly, stroking the old man's hand. 'Don't fret, Grandfather — you did your best to make amends. And you must take comfort from the fact that he knew you had forgiven him. He wrote to you saying he understood and was on his way home.'

Stanley sighed. 'That's what I've been trying to tell him,' he said.

'Let us talk of pleasanter things.' Emily picked the daffodils up. 'I'll put these in water and ring for tea. You will stay, won't you, Stanley?'

He forced a smile. 'How could I refuse such a charming invitation?'

While she was out of the room, he tried to distract his grandfather from the subject of Adam. Whenever the old man questioned him, the memory of the bloated body retrieved from the Thames rose before his eyes and he could not repress a shudder. He'd been too squeamish to do the deed himself, but he'd have to overcome his fastidiousness when he'd identified the drowned man.

As the months had passed he had almost come to convince himself that it had been Adam's body. But his grandfather's constant harping on the subject was beginning to get on his nerves.

The old man lapsed into silence and Stanley gazed out at the terrace and the formal gardens beyond. In the distance the rich farmlands of the estate were showing signs of spring. All this would be his one day — in the not too distant future. He glanced back at his grandfather, who had drifted into sleep. The old man was frail. Surely he couldn't last much longer. The urge to grab a cushion and put it over Justin's face was almost too strong to resist. But not yet. He must be sure of the will before taking such a drastic action.

The door opened and he forced a smile. The maid followed Emily with the tea trolley and he moved a small table next to his grandfather's chair. When Emily poured the tea he placed the cup and saucer on it and urged the old man to try one of the dainty fancy cakes. He could be charming when the occasion demanded.

Emily smiled over the rim of her cup. 'It almost seems as if we are a real family again when you are here,' she said.

He knew she was thinking of her brother and longing for the days before he had been sent in disgrace to work the family's plantation in Jamaica. As he nodded and smiled, forcing himself to indulge in small talk, he inwardly cursed the way his plans constantly seemed to be foiled. He had succeeded in getting Adam banished, but Grandfather had not changed his will.

He had put himself managing the estate and the family's business enterprises in London, trying to prove himself a worthy heir. And he'd thought he was succeeding — until a heart attack had made Grandfather long to see his favourite again before he died. Justin had sent a letter of forgiveness, begging the boy to come home.

If only Stanley had been here then, he would have intercepted the letter. Adam would have ended his days in Jamaica, never knowing that his grandfather wished to make up their quarrel. And Sir Justin would have died believing Adam still bore a grudge.

But Stanley knew the name of the ship his cousin was returning on and he had hired thugs to do his dirty work. Surely with Adam dead, Grandfather would change his will?

As the train steamed through the Kent countryside, anger churned in

Stanley's gut. He couldn't get his grandfather's tears out of his head. Adam was dead, but the old man still favoured him. Something would have to be done before long.

He gazed out of the train window scarcely noticing as green fields and woods gave way to the soot-stained backs of the hovels and tenements on the outskirts of London. His brain was scheming as usual — how to get his hands on the old man's money.

Stanley had received a modest fortune from his father who had died several years ago. But that had almost gone and he needed money badly, especially as he had committed himself to this new venture in London's West End. Suppose Grandfather died without changing his will? Who would inherit now Adam was dead? Would the estate be divided between Justin's heirs? Stanley didn't want to share with anyone — he wanted it all.

A cruel smile twisted his lips. If he

married Emily, he would get her share. She would do for a wife, he could always have a mistress as well. Yes, a mistress — a lady who had fallen on hard times and would be grateful to be set up in a home of her own, knowing that her family were taken care of — Carrie Martin.

As the train pulled into Victoria Station with a hiss of steam, Stanley frowned. As well as telling him who the girl was and where she lived, Budgen had revealed that she already had a protector — a man said to be a cousin who worked for a pittance in the docks. The frown soon disappeared. A poor dock labourer would be no match for Stanley Travers and his money — once he got his hands on it.

Carrie's fingers flew as she stitched the silk flower on to the old worn bonnet.

Nancy sat beside her, watching in admiration. 'I wish I was as handy with a needle as you, love,' she said.

'I'm glad you're not,' Carrie replied,

laughing. 'Otherwise I would have no work to do.'

'Well, since you came to live here, I must be the best-dressed doxie this side of the River.'

Nancy gave a coarse laugh and Carrie smiled too. She had long since ceased to be offended by her friend's outspoken way of speaking and she had accepted that, despite the way she earned her living, Nancy was a good person. She had been forced by circumstance into a way of life that was abhorrent to people of Carrie's former station. But she could not be blamed for that.

After a few more stitches, she cut the thread. 'There, it looks like new,' she said, holding the bonnet up for Nancy to admire.

Nancy put it on and struck a pose. 'Look like a lady, don't I?' she said. She pressed a few coins into Carrie's hand. 'It ain't much. But it's all I've got,' she said.

'I wish I didn't have to charge friends

at all,' Carrie replied.

'You wouldn't have to do this if you took Alf up on his offer,' Nancy said.

'I don't think it's the sort of work I'd be any good at,' Carrie said diplomatically.

'Well, think about it. The offer won't be open forever. And the pay's good.'

As Nancy stood up to leave, Eliza came in from the yard. She was still pale after her last bout of illness and the cough now seemed to be permanent. But her voice was strong as she challenged her sister. 'What was Nancy talking about? Carrie, you're not thinking of . . . ?'

'Of course not. How could you think such a thing?'

'What did she mean then?'

'Alf Budgen and his partner have opened a new gaming club in the West End — a very high-class establishment, Nancy says. She's going to be the hostess, welcoming guests and so on. She says they need a housekeeper, someone to supervise the staff, order supplies, that kind of thing.'

'You could easily do a job like that. After all, you ran our household back in Denton Heath. If you got the job would we be able to afford a better place?' Eliza asked excitedly. Her eyes lit up. 'Oh, Carrie, I could work there too. I could be a maid, or serve refreshments.' She swayed and clutched the edge of the table as the hacking cough racked her body again.

'Eliza, love, sit down. Here, take a drink.' Carrie guided her sister to the chair by the fire and poured a glass of water from the jug on the dresser. 'You're not fit to go outside, let alone take a job. Besides, I couldn't let you be a maid.'

'I don't see why not,' Eliza said through ragged breaths. But her protest was feeble. Carrie knew how she longed to help and tried to comfort her by saying, 'It's no use getting excited. I'm not working for Alf Budgen and that's that. I've seen the way he treats Nancy. Besides, how do we know this club's a respectable place?'

Eliza was too exhausted from coughing to pursue the subject and she sat gazing into the fire while Carrie put her sewing things away and began to prepare an evening meal. John had been working steadily for a few weeks and thanks to him, the rent was paid up to date and there was food in the larder.

Carrie knew she should be grateful for this small improvement in their circumstances but, as she cast anxious glances at her sister, she knew that it was not enough. They had to get out of this damp hovel and find a better place to live, somewhere that was not a stranger to sunshine and fresh air. But they could not rely on a permanent change in their fortunes. John Jones, whatever his real name was, could recover his memory any day now and when he did he would return to his old life and they would be back where they'd been before he came into their lives.

As the days lengthened into spring he

had become stronger physically and he no longer suffered from the blinding headaches that had plagued him, although he still occasionally woke in confusion and terror from nightmares. But most of the time he seemed happy enough, working at the docks and spending his evenings quietly at home. He did not seem to feel the need to join his workmates at the pubs after his day's work.

Carrie and Eliza had decided it was useless to question him about his former life. Instead, they chatted about their own childhood in Kent, the simple pleasures of village life, the occasional treats such as the ball at Lintons. Carrie hoped their seemingly idle chatter would spark off a memory as it had when they'd been talking of music and he mentioned his sister.

Often he would fall silent and sit gazing into the fire, racking his brains for a name, a place, anything that would tell him of his past life. If only she could help him, Carrie thought. But part of her was happy with the way things were. She couldn't bear the thought that one day he would leave them.

A few days later Carrie was crossing the yard to the standpipe when Alf Budgen emerged, yawning and scratching as if he'd just got out of bed. She bent her head, hoping to avoid him but he called across to her.

'Thought any more about my offer? Or are you too stuck up to work for the likes of me?' he gave a coarse laugh.

Carrie's cheeks flamed. He was referring to the housekeeper's job at his West End club but she dreaded what interpretation others might put on his words.

She ignored him, but as she held her pail under the trickle of brownish water from the pipe, she wondered why she was being so stubborn. Nancy had told her that there were servants' quarters in the mansion that was to house the club. What bliss it would be to live once more in a place with running water, maybe even a bath. And Alf had hinted that there would be employment for her father too.

Head held high, Carrie lifted the bucket and marched across the court.

'You'll come round in the end Miss High and Mighty,' Alf said as she passed him.

'Never,' Carrie muttered as she slammed the door. Tempting as it was, she did not trust Alf Budgen and she had a suspicion that once installed in the club her duties would involve more than she bargained for. She didn't care for herself, but she would not expose her young sister to that kind of life.

As for employing her father in a gaming house, she could not imagine a worse plan for him, although he had been staying home more often lately. Carrie suspected his new gambling friends were getting tired of him always owing them money.

He was here now, having stumbled home in the small hours muttering incoherently and fallen asleep in the chair. She ought to wake him and insist that he at least made some pretence of finding work.

If John, who was still far from fully recovered, could contribute to the household, surely Father could make some effort. She sighed and decided to leave him to sleep while she and Eliza went to the market. A little fresh air would do them both good.

They closed the door quietly and hurried across the court and through the narrow alleyway into the main road. Carrie was anxious to avoid another encounter with Alf Budgen.

Eliza had not left the house for days and she clutched Carrie's arm, looking apprehensively at the crowds of ragged children with bare feet and running sores and old women picking rubbish out of the gutters. She cringed closer to her sister as they passed a group of rough-looking foreign seamen lounging on a street corner outside an alehouse.

Carrie had become used to the sights, but as Eliza voiced her horror, she realised they had to get away from here. But she patted Eliza's arm reassuringly. 'Those men are quite harmless. And as for the poor children, it is hardly their fault they have to live this way,' she said.

She did not tell her sister that on several occasions she had eaten fruit and vegetables that had fallen from a market stall and rolled into the gutter. Even when you had no money, you still had to eat. But the habit of protecting Eliza from the harsher facts of life was hard to break. At least today she could buy her vegetables and maybe even a little meat to go with them.

They finished their shopping and Carrie noticed that Eliza seemed tired. But when she suggested they should go home, the younger girl smiled and said, 'Oh, please, not yet. Let's look round the other stalls. I have been so bored shut up in the house for so long.'

'So long as you feel well enough,' Carrie said, noting the colour in her sister's cheeks. The warmth of the spring day certainly seemed to have done her good and Carrie herself was not ready to go home yet. She always dreaded returning to the reality of their life in Brewers Court. Holding her sister's arm and pushing their way between the crowded market stalls, picking up trinkets and ribbons, even though they could not buy them, she could almost believe that they were back in Denton Heath, their maid following behind carrying the basket containing their shopping.

She was brought back to earth with a start when a tall dark man accosted her. 'Miss Martin, I believe.' He raised his hat. 'And the charming Miss Eliza.'

'Do I know you, Sir?' Carrie asked, struggling to remember where she had seen him before. From his clothes and his manner of speaking she knew he was a gentleman. He was handsome with piercing blue eyes, but his lips were thin and his smile did not reach his eyes.

'My apologies — you do not remember me,' he said. 'Stanley Travers. We met not far from here some months ago. We literally bumped into each other but we did not introduce ourselves.'

'Then how do you know my name, Sir?'

'I am a friend of your father's. Josiah and I have, shall we say, interests in common. He told me of his two charming daughters and pointed you out to me. I recognised you straight away as the young lady I had met before.'

'I wonder then why my father did not introduce us at the time,' Carrie said struggling to speak politely.

She could not be rude to a friend of her father's, but she did not like the man or the way he looked her up and down. As soon as he had spoken she had remembered their previous encounter on the day a drowned man had been pulled from the Thames.

At the time she had assumed he was some sort of official. She had not liked him then and her opinion did not change as he continued speaking.

'My apologies if I was a little abrupt at our last meeting.' He lowered his eyes and assumed a solemn expression. 'I was rather distracted as I had just been called upon to identify the body of my cousin. He had been robbed and thrown into the river.'

Eliza gasped and said, 'How dreadful. Our condolences, Mr Travers.'

Carrie recalled that at the time he had not seemed too distressed. Taking Eliza's arm she said, 'Come along, dear. We have more shopping to do.'

Travers raised his hat again. 'Good day, ladies. I must go too. I also have business to attend to.'

He hurried away and Carrie gazed after him. There was something disturbing about the man. Why had he told them about his cousin? There had been no need to raise the subject unless it was to enlist their sympathy.

'I wonder why Father had not mentioned Mr Travers,' Eliza said. 'I had no idea he still had any friends left from before.'

'Maybe they met after we came to London,' Carrie said, still staring after him. He had stopped to speak to somebody and she gasped as she recognised Alf Budgen.

As they left the market and made their way along Wapping High Street towards home, Carrie scarcely listening to her sister's chatter. Stanley Travers must be the *gentleman* Nancy had referred to — the man who was financing Alf's gaming club. And gambling was the link between Travers and her father. Her mind was now made up. She would definitely decline the position Alf had offered her.

Eliza tugged at her sleeve. 'You're not listening, Carrie. I said, what a pleasure it was to talk to a real gentleman for a change. Why did you not tell me when you met him before?'

Carrie almost laughed at her sister's naivety. Just because he spoke in a refined manner, raised his hat and was well-dressed, did not make him a gentleman. She was tempted to tell

Eliza about that earlier encounter when he had gripped her wrist and raked her body with his insolent eyes. And he was doing business with Alf Budgen, a small-time criminal with big ideas.

Carrie Martin was a woman who prided herself on the way she had taken care of her family since the decline in their fortunes, a woman who was not afraid to brave the dark stinking reaches of the River Thames to help provide for them. She had thought there was nothing worse to face. But Stanley Travers' cold smile sent an inexplicable shiver of terror down her spine. She hoped this would be their last encounter.

7

They reached home, Eliza prattling about their meeting with Mr Travers. Carrie didn't want to spoil her sister's pleasure, but if she had her way, neither of them would see Stanley Travers again.

The room was exactly as they'd left it and the fire was almost out. 'You'd think Father would tend to the fire at least,' she complained, furious that he was still sleeping off his drunken bout while she struggled to look after them all.

He was snoring and Carrie shook his shoulder. The room was cold but his face was covered in a sheen of sweat. She touched his forehead and drew back her hand with a gasp. He wasn't drunk, she realised, he was ill.

'Father, what's wrong?' she whispered.

He opened his eyes, glazed with fever, but did not seem to know her.

'Eliza, fetch water quickly — and a cloth. Father's ill.'

Her sister quickly obeyed and they helped him to the couch. 'It may be just the drink, but I fear it's something worse,' she said, covering him with the thin blanket. She took the bowl of water and the cloth and sat beside him, bathing his forehead. He had begun to mutter deliriously, but the cool compress seemed to soothe him and he fell into a deep sleep again.

Eliza watched anxiously. 'Will he be all right?' she whispered.

'I hope so.' Carrie smiled reassuringly. 'We'll let him sleep while we make him a nourishing broth. He'll probably be hungry when he wakes.'

She hoped that keeping busy would stop her sister from worrying. But as they worked they frequently glanced towards the couch. Eliza was uncharacteristically quiet, while Carrie was racked with guilt for her previous uncaring attitude. Father had probably been ill when he came in last night but she had automatically assumed he was drunk.

* * *

John was beginning to get used to his new name and his new life. He could not pretend that working in the docks was an ideal career, but it was a living. And the money he earned enabled him to help the family who had been so good to him. What would have been his fate if Carrie had not found him before the tide turned?

How he admired the girl who had rescued him. As he recovered from his beating and near drowning, she had sat at his bedside, distracting him with stories of their former life and he could only admire the strength that had helped her to make something of the change in their fortunes. She always seemed cheerful, never giving in to the despair she must often have felt when things were at their worst. He hardly dared admit his true feeling for her. Who knows if I have the right to love her, he asked himself.

He quickened his steps as he neared Brewers Court, only longing for the sight of Carrie's face lit up in a welcoming smile after his hard day's labour. And she would have something to smile about today.

His pockets bulged with oranges, hastily scooped up from a burst crate before the overseer noticed. All the dockworkers did it and he had long since learned to stifle his conscience. He also carried a chicken by its scrawny neck, bought from a street vendor, the last of the day going cheap.

Despite the squalor of his lodgings, John was almost happy, and in Carrie's company he often thought that it wouldn't matter if he never regained his memory. He would work hard and maybe one day they would be able to move to better surroundings. He would take care of her and her family as she had taken care of him during his illness.

But he knew it would remain a dream until he remembered his past. Suppose he found he was already married, maybe with children? He felt sure he would know deep down if it were so.

But there was an even greater fear — the reason he had been attacked and left for dead. He had a feeling he was still in danger. It had been no ordinary robbery — the nightmares told him that. Afterwards he would awake terrified, a voice echoing in his ears, speaking of payment for a job well done.

Somebody had hated him enough to pay for his death. A name fluttered at the edge of his consciousness. If only he could remember it, the mystery of his past life would be solved. And a known enemy would be less terrifying.

As he entered the gloomy archway leading to the court, John shook off his sombre thoughts. He did not want to add to Carrie's burden by revealing his fears.

But his smile disappeared when he opened the door and saw Carrie's face. Eliza had been crying too.

'What's wrong,' he cried, dropping the chicken on the table and going to Carrie's side, taking her hand. His first thought was that she or her sister had been assaulted by one of the ruffians who lurked at the entrance to the court.

'Father's ill. He's rambling, delirious . . . '

'Are you sure he's not just . . . '

Carrie snatched her hand away. 'He's not drunk,' she snapped. Her eyes filled with tears and her tone softened. 'That's what I thought at first,' she confessed. 'But he's really ill.'

John went to the old man's bedside. Josiah's face was beaded with sweat and his breath came in ragged gasps. He turned to Carrie. 'We must cool the fever. Keep bathing him with cold water and make sure he has plenty to drink. Broth too, if he will take it. That's what we did when my sister had the fever — and she recovered.'

He turned as Carrie gasped and said, 'What did you say?'

He looked momentarily confused. 'I don't know — it just came into my head.'

'Does this mean you're getting your memory back?'

'Not really — it's just little things, usually when I'm thinking about something else.' He shook his head. 'No matter. We must think of your father now and concentrate on getting him well.'

He helped Carrie to change the sweat-soaked sheet, then sat beside Josiah, bathing his forehead and encouraging him to take sips of water. Watching over the old man, John lapsed into thought, puzzling over the curious way the brain worked.

Twice now he had mentioned his sister but he did not know her name, whether she was grown up and married or still just a girl. He hoped Carrie would not question him about it. It only confused him, bringing those dark thoughts crowding in. He closed his eyes and his mind was filled with darkness, muttered curses, the thud of heavy boots and over it all, the brooding face and cynical smile of a tall, dark man with blue eyes like his own.

There were rumours that the fever running rife in the courts and alleys around Wapping was cholera, some said typhoid. Whatever it was, Carrie learned on one of her rare expeditions to the market, several people in the neighbourhood had already died. She was terrified that Eliza would catch it and hated leaving her alone with their father.

When she reached home, Eliza was crying. 'Thank God you're back, Carrie. He was thrashing about and shouting. And now . . .'

'Please, God, he's not dead,' Carrie whispered, leaning over the couch. She had often been angry and impatient with Josiah lately, but she still loved him. He sprawled on his back, tangled in the sheets, his mouth open, breath rattling in his throat. She stroked the hair back from his forehead and bent to kiss him. She could see the end was not far off.

'Is he . . . ?' Eliza whispered.

'Not yet, but . . . '

'Let me sit with him.'

Carrie nodded. They each took a hand and silently sat with him until John came in. Carrie got up, leaving Eliza to watch over the old man.

John took her hands in his. 'Is he any better?' he asked.

'Worse, I'm afraid.' She felt the tears clogging her throat and when he put his arms around her, she leaned against him, grateful for his strength. 'It won't be long I fear,' she said.

'I'm so sorry, Carrie.'

She sighed and pushed him away. 'You look tired. Sit down and I'll dish up the stew.'

'You should eat too,' John said, when he saw that she'd only set the table for one.

'I can't.' She ladled stew into a bowl and pushed it towards him, sat down at the table, her head in her hands.

'You're tired too,' John said. 'When I've finished this, I'll sit with your father for a while. You both need to rest.'

Carrie watched him eat. Usually he devoured his food, hungry after a hard day at the docks, but today he picked at the food. The scar on his temple had faded now, but he often looked drawn and tired and she wondered if his other injuries still troubled him, especially doing such physical labour.

She had not referred to his flash of memory on the day her father had been taken ill. Questioning only made things worse. But she could not help wondering what his life had been before they met.

He pushed the food away half-eaten and stood up. 'You and Eliza must both eat and rest.'

Carrie filled two bowls with stew and put them on the table, but neither of them ate much, their thoughts with the man they still loved. Although he had not been a perfect father, Carrie knew that, like her, Eliza was recalling happier times before their mother died, when the lovely old house at Denton Health had been filled with love and laughter.

They had both dozed a little, their heads resting on their arms at the table when Carrie jumped up with a start. There had been no sound, but she sensed something was wrong. She glanced across the room where John slumped in the chair, dozing. Josiah's rasping breaths had ceased and he looked younger and more at peace than he had since the death of her mother.

When Eliza started to sob, she put her arms round the younger girl. 'Hush, dear. He's with Mother now,' she whispered.

As she comforted her sister, she realised that John had not stirred. She pushed Eliza away and went to his side, feeling his forehead. 'Oh, no, he's caught it, too. I should have realised he was ill,' she said, recalling how tired he'd looked and that he had refused his food.

⋆ ⋆ ⋆

Between arranging her father's burial and caring for John in his delirium, Carrie had no time to worry about Eliza or herself catching the fever.

Poor Josiah Martin had ended up in a pauper's grave. As she said her farewells, Carrie vowed that if there was a change in their fortunes, he would be reunited with his wife in the pretty village churchyard at Denton Heath.

Now, as she bathed John's forehead and prayed for his recovery, she reflected that such a change was more unlikely than ever. Without John's wages to support them, things were as bleak as they had been the previous winter.

Her thoughts turned to the gold pocket watch still hidden at the back of the drawer. Selling it could mean the difference between survival and starvation. But her conscience would not allow her to dwell on it. If worse came to worst there was still the chance of employment at Alf Budgen's gaming club though she still shuddered at the thought, especially as Nancy had confirmed that the gentleman he had gone into partnership with was the odious Mr Stanley Travers.

John began to mutter deliriously once more, his head turning from side to side on the damp pillow. He kept shouting, 'No,' and trying to push her away just as he had on the night she and Jerry had fished him out of the river. Once he sat up, eyes staring. 'Why won't you believe me, Grandfather?' he asked, a sob in his voice, sinking back on the pillow.

Carrie leaned over him and took his hand, trying to soothe him. He gripped her fingers. 'It's all his doing — he's always hated me.' His voice trailed away into incoherent muttering. But Carrie managed to make out his next words and she let go his hand abruptly. He was calling for his, 'Sweet Emily', heartbroken at the thought he might never see her again.

8

A few days later the fever broke and Carrie knew that John would not die. Her joy was tempered by the knowledge that soon he was sure to remember everything and then he would leave them to return to his 'dear Emily'. But until then she would make the most of every moment.

She clasped Eliza's hands. 'He's going to be all right,' she cried.

Eliza too was overjoyed. 'I could not have borne it if he had died too,' she said.

Carrie looked at her sternly. 'I hope you're not entertaining any foolish notions about our so-called cousin,' she said.

Eliza laughed. 'Of course not — he is like a brother to me.' She gave her sister a playful push. 'Besides, he only has eyes for you, dear sister. I am surprised he has not spoken before now.'

'Now you are being foolish,' Carrie said, smiling. But her heart was breaking. Before his illness she had begun to hope that John returned her feelings. But now she knew his heart belonged to another.

She continued to nurse him, enjoying the bittersweet intimacy while she could. But she knew it could not last and it was almost a relief when at last he was well enough to go back to work. With him out of the house for the greater part of the day it would be easier for her to conceal her feelings.

John had been back at his job for a few days and was beginning to look more like his old self. Before his illness, he and the sisters had often sat together in the evenings talking quietly.

Now Carrie kept herself busy, or excused herself saying that she was tired, afraid that if she spent too much time with him, he would begin to guess how she felt about him — and that would not do now that she knew he loved someone else.

She never spoke of what he had said in his delirium and he never again referred to his 'sweet Emily'. But one day he would remember. The thought was like an arrow in her heart.

He was sitting in her father's old chair, gazing into the fire, smiling at something Eliza had said, while Carrie scoured a blackened cooking pot. He looked up and spoke suddenly. 'I have been thinking that I should leave here.'

'No, you cannot,' Carrie exclaimed without thinking. 'Where would you go?'

'I could find lodgings nearby,' he said.

'But why? Are you not happy with us?'

'I have never been happier,' he said, 'but it is not right for me to be living with two young ladies. What of your reputations?'

Carrie laughed. 'Who cares about such things in this place? Besides, most people have accepted that you are a cousin.' Although she knew it would be for the best, she did not want him to leave.

Eliza added her pleas for him to stay.

He smiled and repeated his determination to find other lodgings.

'You must do as you think best,' Carrie said after a moment. She put the pot on its shelf and came to sit near him. 'We have no right to keep you here.'

John leaned forward as if he would have taken her hand but she moved out of his reach. 'Miss Martin, Carrie, you have cared for me as if I were indeed part of your family and I'm grateful for everything you have done for me. But I cannot continue like this, not knowing who I am or how I came to be here . . . '

His eyes were shadowed and he passed a hand over his face. 'It is time I did something about it. I can't hide in the shadows for ever. I intend to make inquiries along the wharves. Someone must know who meant me harm and I will make them pay for what they did.'

'You believe it was not just a random attack then?' Carrie asked.

'I am convinced of it.'

'Have you remembered something?'

'Just jumbled voices and faces, enough to know that someone hated me and wished me dead. That is why I must not stay here. You could be in danger if that person discovers I am still alive. I would not bring that to your door.'

Now that he had raised the subject, Carrie had to ask. 'Have you remembered anything else — names, places?'

A troubled frown creased John's brow. 'Not really. I get fleeting impressions but they go before I can pin them down.' He turned to Carrie, his eyes alight with hope. 'Why do you ask — did I say anything while I was ill?'

'You talked a lot, mostly nonsense . . . ' She hesitated.

'Yes . . . ?' He nodded impatiently.

'You mentioned that someone hated you, that this person blamed you for something. You swore you were innocent and begged your grandfather to forgive you.'

'I said all this and you did not tell me? Why?'

'You were delirious, your words did not make sense and I thought if I mentioned it, you would only be more confused. I have only now pieced it together from what you have just told me.'

'Maybe you were banished to Jamaica because of what you had done,' Eliza, who had been quietly listening, said.

'Or what someone thought you had done,' Carrie amended, sure that the John she knew could not have been guilty of anything really bad.

'But why? What would make someone hate me so?' He buried his head in his hands. 'If only I could remember.'

Carrie longed to comfort him but instead she stood up and spoke as calmly as she could. 'I am sure that it will all come back to you in time. But please, John, do not think of leaving until you know where your real home is. Eliza and I are not afraid — after all, we have lived in this dreadful place for almost three years now and so far we have not come to any harm.'

John nodded gratefully. 'Thank you — I will stay.'

'I'll wish you goodnight then. Come, Eliza.'

As she undressed and got into bed beside her sister, Carrie wished she'd had the courage to mention the name he had cried out. Surely it would be better for her to know if he belonged to another.

John had left for his work at the docks by the time the sisters were awake. Carrie was relieved, sure that her feelings would show. She carried on with her chores, tidying the shabby room as best she could, wondering what she would say to him when he returned that evening. She was lost in thought when Eliza asked the question that she herself had been reluctant to acknowledge.

'What will happen to us if John does leave?' she asked.

Since their father's illness and death they had been dependent on his contribution to the household. But while he was ill there had been no money coming in and they had fallen behind with the rent. Carrie had had no opportunity to go *mudlarking* and the sewing work had dried up since Nancy had moved away from Brewers Court to live at Alf's West End club.

'We'll manage. I'm sure I can find work,' she said briskly.

'I could work too. I'm so much better now,' Eliza said eagerly.

Carrie smiled. 'I was so relieved that you did not catch the fever. I felt sure you would succumb to it.'

'Like you, I did not have time to be ill.'

Carrie was proud of her little sister who suddenly seemed so grown up. She could not have managed to nurse the sick men without her help. But she still worried that the cough would return.

The recent fine weather had driven the damp from the cottage and that must have helped but she was afraid of what the following winter would bring if their circumstances did not improve before then.

Now that John was working again they should be able to catch up with the rent, but she would have to find work of some kind too. What could she do? She had made a little money sewing for Nancy and her friends, but she was no seamstress. There were factories that employed women nearby and, although she dreaded the thought of working in such a place, she knew she would do if it was really necessary.

'If only Nancy were still here. I could ask her advice,' she said.

'She would tell you to work for Alf Budgen, and you know what that would mean,' Eliza said in her new worldly-wise voice.

'He could have been sincere in wanting a housekeeper,' Carrie said. But she knew she would never ask him for a job if it also meant coming into contact with Stanley Travers.

'Let's not worry about it now. It's a fine day — we could go to the market,' Eliza said.

'Not much point when we have no money,' Carrie said. 'Still, there are a few coppers left. We could buy pies for our dinner.'

'It would be a nice change from stew,' Eliza said.

As they strolled along arm in arm, enjoying the warm spring air and their escape from the dark hovel they called home, Carrie tried to ignore the poverty and squalor around them. When they reached the market in Wapping Lane it became easier as they threaded their way between the colourful stalls and listened to the patter of the market traders.

Passing the pawn shop on the corner of Brewhouse Lane, they paused to peer in the window at the dusty objects on display. There was Carrie's silver locket in among the rings and brooches.

She turned away sadly, knowing she would never have the chance to redeem it now.

The door of the shop stood open and they heard raised voices from inside. 'If I find out it has passed through your hands, it will be the worse for you, my man.'

Carrie pulled at Eliza's arm when she recognised the voice of Stanley Travers and she had no wish to encounter that man again.

The pawnbroker was protesting. 'I gave you my word, sir. If it comes into my possession I will let you know.'

'That watch is a very precious family memento and I intend to find out who stole it from me,' Stanley said. 'And if you had a hand in it you will end up in Newgate.'

Heavy footsteps were followed by the slam of the shop door. At the mention of a watch Carrie's heart began to thump as she remembered what was hidden in the drawer at home. She drew Eliza into a doorway, waiting until the man had gone before daring to resume their walk.

Eliza shook off her sister's hand. 'That was Father's friend, Mr Travers. Why did you avoid him?' she asked.

'He was no friend of Father's. He is a gambler and I believe Father owed him money. He is not a nice man, Eliza, for all he speaks like a gentleman. You heard the way he addressed that poor little shopkeeper. Besides, he is in business with Alf Budgen and I do not trust him.'

They walked along in silence and Carrie went over the conversation they had just heard. Surely the watch she had found could not be the same one? She shook her head. The initials were quite different to Stanley Travers'. Nevertheless, she was relieved that she had resisted the temptation to sell or pawn it. She would not only have been guilty herself but would have got the poor pawnbroker into trouble as well.

They stopped at the bakers in Wapping Lane and bought the pies with the last of their money. Carrie hated ready-made pies, often wondering what Mr Timms put in them. But there was no oven in the tiny cottage, and they mostly lived on stews and broths which she cooked on the open fire.

Stanley Travers stormed his way up Wapping High Street, muttering to himself and ruthlessly pushing his way between the crowds, ignoring the curses that followed him. Nothing seemed to be going right for him.

He had sunk the last of his money into the West End gaming club and it would be a while before he began to see a return on his investment. It wasn't as if he could advertise. He had to rely on word of mouth and it was proving a slow business. Still, he had to congratulate himself on his choice of partner.

An evil grin twisted his lips as he thought of the high-class girls Alf now employed. But the grin was replaced almost immediately by a ferocious scowl. There was one thing Alf had not been able to do, despite his promises.

'But I will have them,' Stanley muttered pushing an old woman into the gutter. The Martin girls, especially the older one, were never far from his thoughts.

His pleasant fantasy was interrupted when a voice hailed him. It was the constable who had been present when he identified the sailor's body as his cousin. His stomach began to churn and he swallowed dryly.

'Mr Travers, Sir, what brings you to these parts? This is no place for a gentleman,' the man said, indicating the squalor surrounding them.

'I had business down at the docks and I thought I would walk back to the City rather than taking a cab,' Stanley replied, hoping the constable would believe his excuse for being in this unlikely place.

'Not a wise decision if I may say so, Sir.'

Stanley nodded, deciding that a little of the truth would not hurt. 'I have another reason for being here.'

He coughed and tried to look solemn. 'When my poor cousin was drowned there were no possessions on his body. He had a watch, an ornate gold pocket watch, engraved with his initials . . . '

'Valuable, Sir? Even when a death is accidental, it's not unusual for those who find the body to rob the poor victim.'

Stanley touched his lips with a handkerchief, then dabbed at his eyes. 'It is not the monetary value, rather the sentimental. It is a family heirloom you see, given to my cousin by my grandfather. The poor old man has almost lost his wits since this tragedy and refuses to believe that Adam is really dead until he sees the watch.' He gave an inward smirk at the convincing break in his voice.

'That's sad, Sir.' The constable took a small notebook from his breast pocket. 'Give me a description of the item and I will see that it is circulated among my colleagues.' He wrote laboriously at

Stanley's dictation and put the book away. 'It may never turn up, Sir, I'm afraid. Even the most daring thieves round here wouldn't touch such a distinctive item — the initials, see. It's probably been melted down for the gold.'

'I have been to every pawnbroker in Wapping and Shadwell, but they all deny seeing it.'

'That doesn't surprise me, Sir.'

The constable accompanied him to the main road and hailed a cab for him. 'Leave it to us, Sir. It's dangerous for a gentleman such as yourself to go making his own inquiries.'

Stanley threw himself into the cab and barked an order at the cabby. 'Silly old fool,' he muttered, leaning back in the seat. He had to find that watch. Once his grandfather saw it, he would have to believe it had been pawned by the thug who'd beaten Adam and thrown him in the Thames to drown. Only then would he accept that his precious grandson was really dead. The old fool would have to change his will then.

As the cab rattled towards the West End, Stanley fumed anew, cursing his own stupidity in not hanging on to Adam's possessions as proof of the body's identity. But he had feared being a suspect if he had been caught with the wallet or the ring. And the thugs he had hired swore they'd never seen the watch.

'More likely one of them stole it,' he said to himself. When they had realised how easily recognised it would be, they'd probably thrown it in the river. He'd just have to find another way to convince the old man, he thought.

He relaxed and once more gave himself up to the Martin sisters. If Budgen didn't come up with the goods soon, he'd pay someone to go along to Brewers Court and abduct the girls — or better still, do it himself.

9

When the sisters reached home, Carrie hurried upstairs, leaving Eliza to fill the kettle and put it over the fire. She hung up her bonnet and shawl and went to the drawer where the watch had remained hidden all these months. She had not even told Eliza about it.

She took it over to the window and traced the entwined monogram with her finger. Despite the ornateness of the lettering which made it hard to decipher, she could see that the first initial was definitely *A* and she sighed with relief. If it had been an *S* her innate honesty would have forced her to approach Mr Travers and tell him how she had come by the watch. But it could not be his. It was just a coincidence.

Remembering some of the items Jerry and his gang of friends had found when they had been out mudlarking it was not so surprising. The strangest objects became lodged in the mud or were washed up by the tide.

As she went to put the watch away it occurred to her that she should make some effort to discover its true owner. She carried it downstairs and showed it to Eliza.

'Do you think it's the one Mr Travers was inquiring about?' her sister asked, fingering the ornate gold case.

'Those are not his initials,' Carrie pointed out.

'Maybe it was left to him by a relative. He said it was a family heirloom,' Eliza said.

'I had not thought of that,' Carrie admitted. 'If it is his we should give it back.'

'Maybe there's a reward.'

'Eliza, you should not think of such things. We should return it because it's the right thing to do.' Carrie took it from her and put it on the dresser. 'I will make some inquiries.' She did not want to approach Stanley Travers herself. When John came home she would ask his advice.

The kettle boiled and she made a pot of tea, using the last of their precious leaves. They did not often indulge these days in what had been an everyday ritual in their former life. As she sipped the refreshing liquid, Carrie's eyes strayed to the gold watch lying on the dresser. She wished she hadn't kept it now. But so much had happened in the past months that she had almost forgotten about it.

When she finished her tea she realised that the water bucket was almost empty. Normally John would refill it when he returned from work, but Carrie tried to stop him doing too much as he was still weak from the fever.

She went out to the standpipe and, while she waited for the bucket to fill, she looked around the dirt yard where scummy water had pooled between the broken flagstones and then up at the sky, hardly visible between the smoking chimney pots. Jerry's little brothers and sisters were playing listlessly in the mud and, as she watched, the door to his cottage opened and he came out.

'Get indoors, you lot. Yer tea's ready,' he shouted, picking the littlest one up and hefting her on to his hip. He looked up and saw Carrie with her bucket.

' 'Ere, Miss, let me carry that for yer,' he said.

'That's all right. I can manage. You see to your sister.' She crossed the yard towards him. 'She looks much better, doesn't she?' The fever had hit Jerry's family hard and one of his brothers had died.

'Yeah — and so does your gent. I see 'e's gone back to work. Lucky it were just a summer fever and not the cholera. We'd all 'ave been gonners then,' he said.

Carrie smiled and opened her door, then turned back. 'Jerry, could you do something for me?'

'Course, Miss.' His eyes gleamed.

'Wanna come mudlarking again? We ain't done that fer a while.'

'No. I need you to ask some questions for me.' She described the watch with its ornate monogram and unusual pattern, but did not tell him why she wanted to find out who owned it.

He was understandably curious. 'There's been a gent asking questions round the pawnbrokers lately,' he said.

'I don't think it's the same one,' she said. 'But can you just keep your eyes and ears open for me. I can't pay you, but there could be a reward.'

'Don't matter. I'll do it fer you, Miss.'

'Be careful, Jerry. I don't want you getting into trouble.'

Indoors, she picked up the watch and tried once more to make out the initials. Was it just a coincidence, she wondered. It must be. She had found it months ago, but Stanley Travers must have lost his more recently, else why would he wait till now to make inquiries?

She wished Nancy were still around to ask for her advice. She might even have heard something of the matter from her clients. Carrie knew that she had sometimes entertained those she called *toffs*. But Nancy had moved out of Brewers Court some weeks ago.

John came in soon afterwards and handed Carrie a few coppers, expressing regret that it was not more. He had only managed to get a couple of hours' work that day. He looked tired and drawn and she worried once more that he was overdoing things after the fever. She poured hot water on the used tea leaves and made him sit down to drink.

'Have a rest while I set the table,' she said.

He insisted on helping and went to the dresser to get the plates. She heard him gasp and looked round to see him with the gold watch in his hand, turning it over and running his hands over the engraving.

'Where did you get this?' he asked in a cracked voice.

'I found it.' Carrie snatched it away from him. 'Truly, I did. Do you think I stole it?'

'Of course not. It's just . . . ' He frowned and rubbed his forehead. 'I thought . . . ' He sat down abruptly.

Carrie rushed to his side. 'Are you all right?'

'Have you remembered something?' Eliza asked.

'Leave him alone, Eliza. Can't you see he's not well,' Carrie snapped.

'I'm not ill, just confused. When I saw the watch lying there, I had a flash of memory. I know I've seen it before . . . ' His voice trailed off.

Eliza shook his arm. 'What did you remember? Tell us.'

'It's no use, it's gone again.' John shook his head.

Carrie frowned at her sister. She knew it was no use badgering him.

He looked up, the watch still in his hands. 'Where did you find it?'

Carrie told him about her mudlarking expeditions with Jerry. 'It was not long after we found you.'

He buried his head in his hands again. 'If only I could remember. But when I try, everything becomes confused again. The little that has come back to me doesn't really mean anything, although I've tried to piece it together.'

'Don't try, John. It only distresses you.' Carrie touched his arm gently. 'Come and sit at the table and let us see if we can guess what Mr Timms has put in his pies today.' It was a poor attempt at humour, but John managed to smile.

★   ★   ★

Carrie pulled her shawl closer about her and shivered as she hurried towards Brewers Court, trying to avoid the puddles, although she wasn't sure why she bothered when her feet were already soaked and freezing, despite the fact that it was early summer. The soles of her shoes were almost worn through and she gave a despairing sigh. How would they get through another winter if she did not find work?

She had spent the day in another fruitless round of the factories, this time going farther afield to Whitechapel, and she was tired and disheartened. But she had to try. They could not continue to rely on John's help. Besides, he had not managed to find regular work since the fever, just a few days casual labour here and there. He was at the docks today, helping to unload a cargo boat.

When he wasn't working he spent the days sitting in her father's old chair, the gold pocket watch in his hands, running his fingers over the engraved letters as if he could read his past in them.

Each day she prayed that she would reach home and find that the riddle had been unlocked, that he would look up with a smile and say, 'I'm not John Jones — I'm . . .'

But on a depressing day like this, it was hard to remain optimistic. His past was connected with the watch, though, she was sure of it. Jerry's inquiries had proved fruitless and she did not know what else to do. If she'd had any spare money she would have had handbills printed asking for information but that was out of the question in their present circumstances.

As she turned under the archway into Brewers Court she bumped into Jerry.

'Good job you're 'ome, Miss,' he said. 'There's a gent at your house bovvering yer sister. I was just comin' ter find yer.'

'Do you know who it is, Jerry?' Carrie tried to stay calm. 'How long has he been there?'

'Jest a few minutes. It's that tall geezer wiv the black 'air, wot 'angs around wiv Alf.'

Who else could it be but Stanley Travers? 'Thank you, Jerry. I'll see to it,' she said. 'Could you wait outside? I may need you to run and fetch Mr Jones.'

'Course, Miss. No bovver.'

Eliza was sitting at the table, twisting

her hands in her lap. She looked on the verge of tears.

Stanley Travers loomed over her, the watch in his hand. 'Do you know the penalty for handling stolen goods?' he asked, his voice quiet, but with a threatening note.

'I hardly think that's relevant, since the watch was not stolen,' Carrie said.

Stanley whirled around to face her.

'Now that you've finished intimidating my sister, perhaps you will explain your presence here.' Carrie held her head up defiantly but she was sure he could hear the rapid thumping of her heart. She held out her hand. 'Give it to me, please.'

'Not until you tell me how you came by it,' Travers said.

'If you explain your interest in the matter and convince me it's any of your business, I'd be happy to tell you.'

Travers looked away, glanced at Eliza still cowering in the chair, licked his lips. He blinked rapidly and Carrie realised he was nervous. Her mistrust of the man deepened. He had something to hide.

He threw the watch on the table. 'Perhaps I should return with the constable.' He stormed out, slamming the door behind him.

Carrie rushed to Eliza's side and put her arms round her. The younger girl burst into tears.

'Thank goodness you came in when you did. I was so frightened,' she sobbed.

'It's all right, dear.' She stroked her sister's hair. 'Why did you let him in? I told you to keep the door locked while I was out.'

'He said he wanted to talk about that job, you know, the housekeeper where Nancy works. And he said about being Father's friend and wanting to do something for his daughters. He seemed quite the gentleman, chatting politely while he waited for you to return.' Eliza sobbed anew. 'When he saw the watch on the dresser, his manner changed completely. I was so frightened.'

'Well, he's gone now ... ' Carrie began, pausing as she heard raised voices from outside. She went to the window and raised a corner of the tattered curtain.

Stanley Travers had hold of Jerry, his silver-topped cane raised threateningly over the boy's head. 'You've been asking questions about a gold pocket watch. I want to know why.'

'Hit me if yer wants, but I ain't tellin' yer nothing,' Jerry spat.

'How dare he?' Carrie muttered, letting the curtain fall.

She went to open the door but Eliza pulled at her arm. Carrie shook her off and opened the door. 'Leave that boy alone,' she demanded.

Travers paused, the cane in mid-air, and swung round. 'Don't interfere, Miss Martin,' he said coldly.

Jerry wriggled, cursing and spitting, but the man did not relinquish his grip.

'Let him go. He has done nothing wrong,' Carrie said firmly.

'Maybe we should let the constable

decide that. I'm taking him to the police station. We'll soon get to the bottom of this.'

Jerry's struggle intensified. 'Don't let 'im, Miss, I ain't done nuffin.'

Carrie was sure it was an empty threat to call the constable. Her suspicions were now truly roused. Maybe, as he'd said to the pawnbroker, the watch was a family heirloom left to him by a relative. That would explain the different initials. But since John had seen it she had become convinced that it was connected to his accident and loss of memory. What was Stanley Travers' interest in all this?

He raised the cane one more and she took a step forward, shaking off Eliza's restraining hand, rushed at him, grabbing his arm. He let go of the boy and pushed her. She stumbled and fell to the ground, dazed. He loomed over her and she cringed away, terrified now. 'I told you not to interfere,' he snarled as the cane descended.

But the blow never fell. From the

corner of her eye she saw a figure emerge from beneath the arch and launch itself at Travers with a roar. She scrambled to her feet as the two figures tumbled to the ground, wrestling in the mud and slime. It was John.

Carrie retreated to the doorway, hugging Eliza and trying to calm her sobs. Jerry had disappeared and she hoped he had gone inside his own house. It was too much to hope that he had run for the constable. She did not know what to do, but she couldn't let the fight continue. John was no match for his burly opponent, weakened as he was from illness and poor diet.

Travers pinned him to the ground, his hands round his throat, and banged his head against the stone flags. Carrie started forward, a protest on her lips. She must do something.

As she did so, Travers' grip loosened and his face paled. 'You,' he said hoarsely. 'You're supposed to be dead.'

John coughed, shook his head and smiled grimly. 'No, dear cousin, as you see — I am very much alive.' With renewed strength he pushed Travers away. But the fight was not over yet.

Several people had come out of their houses to watch. No-one seemed inclined to separate the two men, despite Carrie and Eliza's pleas. These rough Eastenders loved a fight. But one of the neighbours, who worked with John at the docks, realised that he was getting the worst of it, and decided that he wasn't going to let the *toff* hurt his mate.

'Oi, leave 'im alone. You've done enough damage,' he shouted.

One of the women joined in. 'Yeah, we don't want your sort 'ere.'

They pulled Travers away, his immaculate clothes streaked with mud, his knuckles bruised and bleeding. He swayed, glaring defiantly at the circle of watchers, then turned and stumbled away. At the entrance to the court he stopped. 'You'll hear more of this, I promise you. Thieves and ruffians, the lot of you,' he sneered.

The crowd burst into raucous laughter and a gang of small boys ran after him, jeering.

Carrie helped John to his feet and led him indoors, followed by her sister. Blood streamed from a cut over his eyes and she eased him into the armchair. Eliza fetched water to bathe his wounds. He leaned back, eyes closed while Carrie dabbed at the cuts and bruises.

As she rinsed the cloth, his eyes flew open and he gazed at her in confusion. 'What am I doing here?' he asked. He tried to struggle to his feet. 'I must get home . . . ' The effort was too much and he sank back in the chair.

'You're hurt. You must rest a while. Then you can go home.' It was an effort for Carrie to say the words. How could she let him go, knowing she might never see him again? But she had always known that when he regained his memory he would go back to his old life. What was there for him here but poverty and hard labour?

Eliza gave a little sob. 'Poor John. I wonder why Mr Travers hates him so — I thought he was going to kill him,' she whispered.

John sat up. 'Travers is a lying, cheating . . . I hate him too.' his eyes flitted frantically round the barely furnished room, then at the sisters, his eyes clouded. 'Who is John? And who are you?'

Carrie laid a hand on his arm. 'You've been ill and we have been looking after you. We did not know your name so we called you John. It is good to see you well again, although getting into a fight is no way to hasten your convalescence.' She smiled, though it cost a great effort, and told him their names.

When he showed no recognition, Eliza started to speak, but Carrie shook her head. She thought it better to say nothing of his loss on memory and how he had stayed with the Martins.

'I thank you for taking care of a

stranger, but I really must be on my way. My family is expecting me home and they will be concerned at my continued absence.'

'Of course. But rest for a while. Do you have far to travel, Mr . . . ?'

'Rosebury — Adam Rosebury. I live in Kent, a small manor in the village of Lower Chilton, a few miles outside Canterbury. I have been abroad, Jamaica, and was on my way home.' he paused. 'You say I have been ill?'

'You were attacked and robbed, left for dead. Then you caught a fever. We thought you might die. You are still a little weak and confused. Maybe you should leave it a little longer before travelling.'

Carrie turned away and busied herself helping Eliza to prepare a meal. 'At least have something to eat first.' Anything to keep him here a little longer. She wanted to ask about his family but dreaded hearing that the Emily of his delirious rambling was his betrothed or, worse still, his wife.

She picked up the watch and handed it to him. 'This must be yours,' she said. 'I found it near where you were attacked.'

He smiled and turned it over. 'My grandfather gave it to me on my twenty-first birthday. I'm glad it was not stolen.'

'Mr Travers seemed to think he had some claim to it,' Carrie said.

'He thinks he has a claim to everything that's mine.' A shadow passed across his face and he started out of his chair. 'He said he thought I was dead. Why would he say that? I must go. Grandfather, Emily . . . '

A knife twisted in Carrie's heart as she saw the grief and confusion on his face. But what could she do? She only wanted his happiness and he would not be happy until he was reunited with his family.

'At least stay here tonight. You will be more fit to travel in the morning. One more day cannot hurt when you have been away for so long.'

Carrie smiled when he agreed, although she knew she was only prolonging the agony of his departure.

10

Jerry watched Stanley Travers wipe the blood from his bruised knuckles with an immaculate handkerchief, then brush ineffectually at the mud on his clothes. He followed the man towards the main road, hurrying closer as he hailed a hansom, barking his orders at the cabbie.

He sprinted forward and leapt on to the back of the cab, clinging to the lamp bracket as it swung round the corner towards the Tower of London. He crouched down, praying the cabbie would not spot him. One flick of that whip and he'd be lying in the road.

It was a risk worth taking, he thought. He'd known little kindness in his life and would not have understood the word loyalty, but that is what he felt towards the Martin family. Carrie had shared everything she found when out mudlarking, Eliza was always sweet and kind, and Mr Jones, when he was in funds, had given treats to his little brothers and sisters. Jerry remembered the oranges he'd brought them when his little sister was sick, saying that the juice was good for the fever.

Now, as he clung on to the swaying carriage, he was determined to repay their kindness by finding out what the toff was up to. As the hansom turned into the Strand, he realised that they were making for the Soho club where Nancy and Alf now lived.

He'd gone there once before asking for work, but Nancy had sent him away saying it was no place for a young lad. If anyone wanted to know why he was there this time, he could say he was still looking for work.

The cab went over a pothole and Jerry almost fell from his precarious perch. He hung on grimly, wondering why Travers had fought the man who'd called him cousin. It must be something to do with that gold watch, he thought.

When Carrie had asked him to make inquiries, he'd learned that Travers had been asking about it, too. But it didn't belong to him. Jerry couldn't read, but he knew the pattern on the back spelled out the owner's name and it wasn't Stanley Travers. He'd heard Travers telling Alf that it had belonged to his cousin and been left to him in his will. But Mr Jones wasn't dead. Jerry recalled the hatred on Travers' face when he had recognised the man he called cousin.

The cab turned into a street of handsome buildings with pillared entrances and large bay windows and Jerry jumped down, hanging back until Travers had paid the cabbie. When the uniformed doorman was busy, he slunk down the area steps into the basement kitchen where the maids prepared food, their faces red with steam and heat from the fire.

Appetising smells made his stomach rumble but he ignored it and crept towards the back stairs. He had to find

Nancy before he was thrown out. She had to help — after all, she was supposed to be Carrie's friend.

He emerged into a wide corridor with doors opening off each side. Through the glass-paned front door, he could see the broad shoulders of the doorman. A staircase curved upwards and above him the crystals of an elaborate chandelier winked in the light of hundreds of candles. But Jerry had no eyes for his surroundings.

He crept forward, his feet sinking into the deep carpet, until voices from above sent him scurrying for cover. A door to his right stood open and he darted inside, ducking down behind one of the sofas that flanked the fireplace.

'Can I fetch you anything — wine, brandy?'

It was Nancy's voice and Jerry almost revealed his presence. But he curled up even smaller when he heard Travers' reply. 'Leave us alone, woman. We have business to discuss.'

The door closed and Jerry held his breath as someone approached, letting it out slowly as the man threw himself into the seat. 'Now, Budgen, what have you to say about this business? You must have known the man was there all this time,' Travers said.

'T'ain't my fault. As far as I knew, my men did the job they were paid for. As for the gentleman stayin' with his sisters, they said he was a cousin. How could I connect the two — you didn't.'

'There is still the matter of your men's incompetence, and the watch. How did Miss Martin come by it, I wonder — especially as I had instructed you to pass over any valuables my cousin might be carrying.'

'I gave you the wallet and the ring, they swore that's all there was.' Alf paused a moment. 'Most likely one of 'em decided to 'ang on to the watch, extra payment like. When he realised it was easily recognised, he chucked it away.'

'And Miss Martin found it? A strange

coincidence,' he murmured.

'That's all it was,' Alf protested.

'Well, it looks as if all my plans have gone awry. My cousin is still alive and the Martin sisters still have their protector, but not for long.' Stanley's cold chuckle sent a chill down Jerry's spine and he hunched lower behind the sofa, holding his breath.

'What do you mean?' Alf asked.

'You and your men will return to Brewers Court to finish the job they bungled. And bring the Martin sisters here as we planned. You can do what you like with the young one, but Miss Carrie is mine.' He chuckled again.

'A touch of the wildcat about that one, a challenge.' Alf did not reply and Stanley barked impatiently, 'Well, go on, man — there's no time to lose. Now that dear Adam has recovered his senses he'll be off to Canterbury, crying to his grandfather. And if I go down for this, I'll take you with me.'

'Don't worry, Travers. I've as much at stake as you. But it'll take a while to get hold of my men.'

Jerry felt the springs of the sofa move as Stanley stood up and he tensed for flight, relaxing as both men crossed the room. When the door closed he stood up cautiously, trying to decide what to do. Much of what they'd said made little sense to him, but he knew Carrie was in danger. He had to warn her.

His first instinct was to get back to Wapping, hitching a ride on the back of another cab if he could. But even that would take too long. As he hesitated, the door opened and he dived behind the sofa again.

★ ★ ★

Carrie lay sleepless, trying to piece together the story of John, or Adam as she must now think of him, and Stanley Travers, the watch, and the mysterious Emily, a name muttered in delirium, then never mentioned again.

There was so much she wanted to ask, but as she had prepared a meal,

Adam sat at the table, watching her with a puzzled expression. He had politely thanked her for looking after him during his illness. But it was the politeness of a stranger.

'He seems to have forgotten us,' Eliza whispered. 'We should tell him . . . '

'No, it will only confuse him. We do not want him to lose his senses again. We must just be thankful that soon he will be restored to his family,' Carrie replied, although she was bursting with questions.

As they sat at table to eat, she tentatively mentioned Stanley Travers again. 'Your cousin seems to have some grudge against you. He did not seem overjoyed to find you alive.'

'He probably hoped to inherit my grandfather's estate, since he has already gambled away most of what his father left. He must have been delighted when he heard that I had not returned from Jamaica as planned.'

'At least your grandfather and the rest of your family will be delighted that you are well,' Carrie said, hoping that he would speak more of them.

But he became agitated again and pushed his plate away. 'I must get home,' he muttered. He stood up and he swayed on his feet.

Carrie helped him to the couch. 'Rest first,' she insisted.

Now, she turned over in bed, carefully so as not to disturb Eliza. Grey dawn showed through the thin curtains and she got up, pulling her shawl around her. She crept downstairs and checked there was water in the pail before making up the fire which still held a few embers from the night before. She filled the kettle and put it over the flames, glancing towards the couch in the corner.

A gasp escaped her lips as she realised it was empty, the blanket folded neatly, his coat gone from behind the door, and the watch no longer on the dresser where he had left it last night. He had gone without a word. She slumped at the table and began to sob.

Jerry was still behind the sofa. The toff was back, there was the chink of glasses, laughter, lewd talk. Would they never go?

He must have dozed off. It was quiet now and he cautiously stretched his cramped limbs. Someone was moving around, collecting glasses, straightening cushions. Steps approached the sofa and he held his breath as they continued towards the window. A hand stretched up to draw back the curtains. He scrambled backwards, gazing up in terror, relaxing as he recognised Nancy.

'What the heck are you doin' here, you little varmint?'

'It's me — Jerry,' he gasped as she grabbed hold of him by the collar.

'So it is.' She let go and gave him a little push. 'Thought I told yer, there's no work here. You weren't after pinchin' something were yer?'

'You know I ain't no thief,' Jerry protested. 'I was lookin' fer you, if you must know, but Alf and that toff came in and I 'ad to hide.' He pulled at Nancy's sleeve. 'You've got to help them.'

'Who? What yer on about?'

'Miss Carrie and her sister. And the gent what's been livin' wiv em.'

'The cousin?'

'He ain't their cousin. That's what they told everyone. But he's in danger. The toff, Mr Travers, he paid someone to kill 'im. Alf's sending his blokes after him.'

'I don't care about him. What about Carrie — what's she to do with all this?'

'Travers told Alf to being them both 'ere.'

'So, she decided to take the house-keeping job after all?'

'I don't know what yer talkin' about, Nancy. Anyway, it ain't housekeepin' he's got in mind fer them girls, take it from me.'

When Nancy's face blanched, Jerry sighed with relief. Now she realised how serious things are. He looked out of the window, shifting impatiently. It was daylight already. 'Well, yer gonna do anything or not?'

Nancy grabbed his arm, marching him to the door. 'Come with me,' she said.

'Where we going? You ain't gonna tell Alf I was here, are yer?'

'Course not. Skip down the back-stairs and wait fer me in the area. Don't let anyone see yer. I'll get the doorman to call me a cab and then we can be on our way.'

Jerry had never ridden inside a hansom before but, as they bounced over the cobbles towards Wapping, he thought it wasn't much different from hanging on the back. Besides, he was too anxious about Carrie to enjoy the experience.

11

It was market day and the narrow streets of Canterbury were crowded with people and animals. Adam looked around, smiling at the thought of the joy and surprise on Emily's and Grandfather's face when he walked in.

He passed the Cathedral and made his way towards the towers of the West Gate. It was only two miles to Chilton Manor. He could walk. He breathed in the country air, so different from the smoky London atmosphere. Home at last. His steps quickened as he glimpsed the twisted red brick chimneys of the manor house through the trees.

Emily was in the garden, picking flowers. She looked round and the blood left her face. She swayed, almost falling as he rushed to support her. As they clung to each other, weeping and asking each other disjointed questions, he realised he should have let them know he was coming. If this was how his unexpected return affected Emily, what would the shock do to his grandfather?

He led his sister to a seat under a tree and sat beside her, clasping her hands and looking into her eyes. 'I'll tell you the whole story later. But first, Grandfather. Is he well?'

'He's still grieving. Cousin Stanley told us it was you . . . ' She broke off, a hand over her mouth. 'We had a service in the village church.'

'You mean that someone is actually buried here?'

Emily laid a hand over his. 'You must not blame our cousin. He said the body . . . ' She stumbled over the word, then recovered. 'The body was badly disfigured.'

Adam bit his lip, remembering Stanley's fury when he recognised him, the muttered threats as he banged his head against the stone flags. His cousin wanted him dead, had paid someone to kill him. Identifying a stranger's body had not been a genuine mistake, but he would not disillusion his gentle sister just yet. He sighed. What had he ever done to Stanley to arouse such hatred?

Emily stood up and took his hand. 'We must go and tell Grandfather you're home,' she said.

'You don't think you should prepare him first? Won't the shock be too much for him?'

'I think his joy will overcome the shock,' Emily said, laughing. 'You know, he always said you would return, even after the funeral. We thought he was having delusions, but he was so sure.'

They walked through the gardens arm in arm, looking up as they neared the house to see the old man coming towards them, a smile of welcome shining through the tears streaming down his face.

Adam was exhausted, overwhelmed by his reception — not only from his grandfather, but the servants and estate workers who crowded to see him, to shake his hand, to add their words of welcome. Last time he'd been here they'd turned their faces away. He'd been in disgrace — Stanley's doing it again. Angry that no one believed him, he'd stormed away down the drive, determined never to come back.

When Grandfather had realised his mistake and begged him to come home, it had taken a long time before he'd been able to swallow his pride and write back.

As he and Emily and the old man sat into the night talking it over, things fell into place.

'I realised Stanley was at fault, almost as soon as you'd gone. But he swore he never meant you to take the blame,' Sir Justin said. 'And he was so pleased you were coming home, even went up to London to meet you.' He shook his head. 'He was devastated when he heard you were dead. He told me he wished he'd had a chance to make amends. Well, he'll be able to now.'

Adam did not reply. How could he

tell the grandfather he loved that Stanley had paid to have him killed? How could he hurt this gentle old man, who had already suffered so much?

He stood up and sighed. 'I think I'll go to bed, Grandfather. It's been a long day.'

Sir Justin embraced him. 'We'll have a proper welcome home party when you feel up to it.'

But as he lay in bed, trying to sleep, a welcome home party was the last thing on his mind. He should be happy now, home with his loved ones at last, safe from his treacherous cousin's scheming, at least for the moment. But that wasn't the reason for his insomnia.

He closed his eyes and saw the serious face framed by dark curls, the brown eyes gazing worriedly into his as she bathed his forehead, her sweet smile when she realised he was conscious. 'Carrie,' he whispered as he drifted into sleep, knowing that he had to see her again.

Carrie slumped at the table, exhausted from crying. When a knock came at the door, hope flooded through her. He'd come back. But John, Adam, wouldn't knock.

She got up cautiously, hoping it wasn't the landlord demanding his rent, laughing with relief when she saw Nancy and Jerry standing outside.

'How lovely to see you, Nancy. Do come in,' she said. 'Have you come about the job?' It occurred to her that now Adam was gone, she would have to support her sister somehow and Nancy turning up now seemed an omen.

'Forget the job,' Nancy said, casting a nervous glance over her shoulder.

Jerry pushed past her into the room. 'Where's the gent?' he asked.

'Mr Jones has left us, gone back to his family,' Carrie said. 'What do you want with him?'

'They're comin' to kill 'im,' Jerry said dramatically.

Nancy put a hand on his shoulder, looking up as Eliza came down the stairs, her face white. 'You're frightening the ladies, love. Let's all sit down.'

Carrie led her sister to the table and they sat close together clutching each others' hands. 'Has he really gone?' Eliza asked.

'He left before I got up. I assumed he'd returned to Kent. But now ... ' Tears filled her eyes and she looked pleadingly at Nancy.

'I'm sure he's safe, love,' her friend said. 'Alf was with me all night and he was still sleepin' off the booze when I got up. Travers is too lily-livered to do the job himself. Alf's gonna hire the same two he used the last time ... '

Eliza gasped and Carrie put an arm round her shoulders. She looked at Nancy. 'I always thought it was a robbery, that John, Adam, was a chance victim. But why ... ?'

Nancy shrugged. 'The usual — money. Somethin' to do with a will.'

Jerry nodded eagerly. 'I 'eard 'im, Miss. He 'ates Mr Jones.'

'Pray God he's reached his home

safely,' Carrie murmured. No wonder he had left without a word. He had to let his family know he was safe, and he must have known that Travers would try to track him down. Had he been trying to protect them by leaving so abruptly? A little of the sorrow that weighed down her heart lifted.

'That's not all, Carrie, love,' Nancy said. 'That job Alf mentioned, it was just a way to get you both to the club.' She hesitated, glancing at Eliza. 'I don't know how to say this . . .'

'I think I can guess. It did seem too good to be true,' Carrie said.

'Should we try to warn Adam?' Eliza asked.

'I'm sure he can take care of himself, now that he knows the truth about his cousin. He should be safe enough, back with his family.' She swallowed the threatening tears at the thought of his joyful reunion with the unknown Emily.

But she told herself firmly that his happiness was more important than her own. She looked up and said to Nancy,

'I know you don't think much of the police, but I think you should report what you know — you too, Jerry.'

Jerry backed away towards the door. 'Oh, no, Miss. I ain't goin' to no police station.'

'It would help Mr Jones, Rosebury, I mean.' It was still hard to think of him by his real name. Carrie looked from Nancy to Jerry, her eyes pleading. 'I'll come with you.' She sighed with relief when both of them nodded reluctantly.

Adam woke from a fitful sleep and dressed quickly. Emily was already downstairs but Grandfather was still asleep.

'What shall we do today?' Emily asked turning towards him with a bright smile, full of love.

'I must return to London,' he said abruptly.

'But you've only just come home. Grandfather will be upset . . . '

'I must go. That girl I mentioned, the one who looked after me . . . '

'Carrie Martin, yes. What about her?'

'I left without thanking her.' It wasn't what he wanted to say. 'You will explain to Grandfather, won't you?'

Emily smiled knowingly. 'I do believe my big brother's in love,' she teased.

'Yes, I am,' he said seriously. 'I don't know if she feels the same, but I intend to find out.'

'Why the hurry? Surely you can wait till Grandfather comes down.'

'I can't, Emily. I have this terrible feeling that she might be in danger.'

The sergeant behind the desk at the police station had known Nancy when he'd been a constable on the beat and at first he was inclined to dismiss the accusations of what he thought were a couple of doxies and a ragged gutter-snipe.

But Carrie hushed the others and proceeded to explain what had happened in her quiet lady-like voice and managed to impress on him how serious it was.

'Mr Rosebury has returned to Kent to reassure his family that he is well.

But we know that Mr Travers will not let the matter rest. He had hired thugs to kill his cousin and is furious that their earlier attempt failed. You must do something,' she said, clasping her hands on the high counter and gazing earnestly at him.

The sergeant took careful notes, then cleared his throat. 'I shall communicate with my superiors and let them decide. My colleagues at the Soho station will probably raid the club you mention. From what you say, they are breaking the law. That will give us an excuse — and if Mr Travers and Budgen are on the premises, they will be arrested.'

Nancy drew in a sharp breath and Carrie laid a warning hand on her arm. She thanked the sergeant and led her friends outside. 'I'm sorry, Nancy,' she said. 'I did not want to implicate Alf, since I know he is your partner, but . . . '

'I don't care about Alf. After the way he's treated me, he can rot in jail for all I care,' Nancy said, 'But I can't go back to the club now can I? For the first time in me life I had a decent place ter live.' She gave a short laugh. 'Didn't last long, did it? Oh well . . . ' She shrugged.

'You can stay with us. Eliza and I would be delighted, wouldn't we? It's not much of a place, but . . . '

'You're a gem, gel,' Nancy said with a catch in her voice. She recovered and laughed. 'It's not as if I ain't used to it.'

They reached Brewers Court and Jerry ran ahead, disappearing into his own house with a wave of farewell.

As they entered the house, they heard footsteps crossing the room above.

Eliza clutched Carrie's hand. 'Is it Alf and those men?'

Nancy laughed aloud. 'He does his dirty work after dark. Anyway I ain't scared of him.' She went to the foot of the stairs and shouted. 'Come down, whoever you are.'

The three women clung together, laughing with relief when Adam appeared. He looked relieved too. 'Thank God, I thought something had happened to you.'

Nancy closed the door and shot the bolt, 'Just in case,' she said.

They all began talking to once, until Nancy hushed them. 'Let Mr Jones, sorry, Mr Rosebury, speak.' She turned to Adam. 'Why have you come back — and what about this business with my Alf and that cousin of yours?'

The shadows lengthened and the room grew dark as the stories were told, finishing with their visit to the police station and the hope that before too long Stanley and Alf would be safely under lock and key.

During the telling, Carrie's eyes never left Adam's and she could hardly wait to ask again the question that Nancy had asked. 'Why did you come back?'

'I realised I had left without telling you, I love you,' he said quietly.

Nancy coughed loudly and stood up. 'I think it's time you and me went to bed, Eliza,' she said, pulling the younger girl to her feet.

When they were alone, Adam led her to the couch and drew her down beside him, his arm around her shoulders. 'I've wanted to say that for a long time,' he said, kissing her gently. 'But I couldn't until I knew who I really was, that I was free to love you. Please tell me you feel the same.'

'Oh, Adam, you know I do.'

He pulled her to him and kissed her again, more passionately this time, but she drew away.

'I do love you, Adam, but are you sure you're free to love me?'

'I would not be here if it were not so,' he protested.

'What about Emily?' she asked, hating herself for asking.

To her surprise he began to laugh. 'Oh, Carrie, my sweet, Emily is my sister.' He stopped laughing and took her hands. 'All this time you've been thinking . . . ?'

'When you were ill with the fever, you called her name and asked her to forgive you. I thought . . . '

'I'm so sorry, my love.' He pulled her to him again and for a while there were no words as they expressed their emotions in kisses and tender caresses.

At last Adam released her. 'I don't think it is wise for me to stay. I should find a lodging for the night.'

'I want you to stay,' Carrie said, smiling at his expression. She stood up. 'I will join my sister and Nancy upstairs. You will stay down here. I will feel safer with you in the house.'

None of them slept very well that night, alert for the sounds of someone breaking in. Despite the assurances of the police sergeant, they could not be sure his superiors had acted on his information.

Adam woke first, and just as he had when he was still plain John Jones, he brought in the coal, filled the water bucket and set the kettle over the fire.

The three women came down shortly afterwards and bustled about preparing breakfast. When they were seated at the table Adam looked round at them. 'I have a proposal to make to you all,' he said.

Carrie blushed and he smiled at her. 'I have already made a formal proposal to Miss Martin,' he said with a grin. 'And she has honoured me by consenting to be my wife.'

Eliza and Nancy exclaimed with delight, subsiding into quiet smiles as Adam continued. 'It's clear you can't stay here. It is too dangerous.'

He told them of the cottage on the estate where they could all stay until after the wedding. 'Nancy too?' Eliza asked.

'Of course. When Carrie joins me at Chilton Manor, you will need a companion.' He turned to Nancy. 'I hope you agree. I had gained the impression you were not anxious to return to your old life?'

'Cor love us, yer ain't wrong,' Nancy exclaimed, then began to giggle. 'Oh, lor, looks like I'll have to learn to talk like a lady, don't it?'

* ★ ★

A year later, on a warm summer day, Carrie and Emily pushed the perambulator across the grass towards The Lodge where Eliza and Nancy were weeding the flowerbed in front of the cottage. Little Amelia, named after Carrie's mother, was fast asleep, her rosy cheeks just visible above the soft blanket.

They went into the cottage and Nancy prepared tea, spreading a snowy cloth over the table and bringing in a plate of the scones she had baked that morning.

In a relaxed carefree atmosphere the four women gossiped together, safe in the knowledge that Stanley Travers and Alf Budgen were locked away and unable to do further harm.

'Grandfather wants to know when his two favourite ladies are going to visit,' Emily said, smiling.

They promised to walk back to the big house after tea and sit with the old man for a while. The restoration of his favourite grandson and delight in a new great-grandchild had done much to counteract the old man's sorrow over Stanley's treachery. He had gained a new lease of life with the addition of so many young people to the household and now took more interest in running the estate with Adam than he had for years.

Eliza too was restored to health, the racking cough long since gone due to the fresh country air and nourishing food from the estate's home farm. But there was another reason for the bloom on her cheeks and the sparkle in her eyes.

The Martins had renewed their acquaintance with the Lintons and Thomas Linton frequently found excuses to ride over to Lower Chilton. And Eliza with her *companion* returned the visits. Denton Heath was not so very far away when you had a carriage at your disposal.

Amelia woke and Carrie picked her up. As she cradled her daughter she looked round at her family with a sigh of contentment. How thankful she was that, despite their poverty, she had not fallen into temptation and sold the precious pocket watch. She was convinced it had played its part in helping Adam to recover his memory and thus led to her present happiness.

She heard footsteps on the flagged path and she rushed to the door into Adam's arms. A year of marriage had not dimmed their passionate love for each other. She smiled up at him and her heart gave that delicious lurch as his blue eyes smiled into hers, just as it had all those months ago when he had lain, bruised and battered on her father's couch.

As she leaned against him, the gold pocket watch, which he now always carried in his waistcoat pocket, pressed against her — a precious heirloom indeed.